"Do you want t̶ make love to me?"

Tyler stared at Revel for an unnerving second, his eyes glinting greenly with the turmoil her question caused. "Damn you—yes!" The hoarse admission seemed wrenched from him and, as if unable to help himself, he pulled her close. His mouth moved across hers in a hard and searing kiss that vividly displayed an uncontrollable hunger, which Revel was shaken to discover promptly kindled an answering craving within herself. Beneath the fierce demand of his lips, hers parted willingly, her tongue licking against his own as it ravaged the moist, sweet recesses made available to it.

Then, just as abruptly as he had drawn her close, Tyler now set her away from him.

"I just wish to hell I didn't, that's all," he groaned on a thickened, uneven note edged with self-disgust. "An entanglement, of any kind, with a protester—" his jaw tightened "—particularly a devious one, is the last damn thing I need or want."

Kerry Allyne developed wanderlust after emigrating with her family from England to Australia. A long working holiday enabled her to travel the world before returning to Australia where she met her engineer husband-to-be. After marriage and the birth of two children, the family headed north to Summerland, a popular surfing resort, where they run a small cattle farm and an electrical contracting business. Kerry Allyne's travel experience adds much to the novels she spends her days writing—when, that is, she's not doing company accounts or herding cattle!

Books by Kerry Allyne

CAUSE FOR LOVE
Kerry Allyne

Harlequin Books

TORONTO • NEW YORK • LONDON
AMSTERDAM • PARIS • SYDNEY • HAMBURG
STOCKHOLM • ATHENS • TOKYO • MILAN
MADRID • WARSAW • BUDAPEST • AUCKLAND

Original hardcover edition published in 1992
by Mills & Boon Limited

ISBN 0-373-03235-8

Harlequin Romance first edition December 1992

CAUSE FOR LOVE

CHAPTER ONE

'COME with us. Really make your voice heard—now—before it's too late and these people destroy the forests at Mount Winsome for ever!' Sebastian Renwick had urged Revel persuasively after the last of several of his environmental meetings that she had attended and, not only fired with enthusiasm by his prior oratory but also as a result of their growing friendship, she had impulsively agreed to his suggestion.

It *was* time to actually stand up and be counted, she had decided. For a while now she had felt the stirrings of concern over what she had read and seen regarding the environment. Consequently, when some spur-of-the-moment whim had initially directed her to Sebastian's meetings, and she had listened to his powerfully delivered arguments and then met him afterwards, his sentiments had suddenly struck a receptive chord within her.

Although now, as Revel prepared to leave to join the other protesters wanting to halt the logging in the Mount Winsome State Forest, some one hundred-and-twenty-odd miles north-west of Brisbane, she found it had been far easier to yield to Sebastian's urgings that she physically demonstrate against what was taking place than it was to convince her sedate, society-matron mother of the necessity for such non-conformist action.

'But why do you, personally, have to go, darling?' queried Isabel Ballard bewilderedly as she watched from the columned portico of their spacious colonial Ascot home while her daughter carried a couple of holdalls down to her car, which was parked on the gravelled driveway at the foot of the wide steps. 'And if it comes to that, why on earth would you want to, particularly if it entails spending the remainder or even part of your holiday in such a fashion?' she continued. Only earlier that same week had Revel begun her yearly four-week break from her hectic and hard-won position as her father's assistant in the family stockbroking concern of Ballard Investments. 'I mean, surely if you feel you must make some sort of protest—although goodness only knows why you should—isn't there a somewhat less extreme manner in which you could do so? Perhaps if you lobbied some of your and your father's associates, or—or even Quentin's, since it seems to me it's really a political matter.'

Looking back at her parent, Revel made a wry face. Her brother, Quentin, at twenty-eight her elder by six years, was generally being touted as an up-and-coming member of one of the major political parties with a good chance of pre-selection at the next State election.

'Except that, these days, politicians only ever seem to take notice of what the people want when there's such a hue and cry they can't ignore them any longer,' she quipped.

Isabel Ballard placed a hand to her chest in a shocked gesture. 'Oh, no, I'm sure you're wrong, darling. And especially where Quentin's concerned.' She drew herself up to her tallest, her bosom swelling. 'In fact, you make me quite angry even insinuating such a thing regarding your own brother, when you know as well as I do that there's no one who's more honest and caring than he. Why, look at all the time and effort he put in to enable——'

'Yes, Mum—I know, I know,' Revel interrupted placatingly, sensing that her evidently indignant mother was about to enumerate every one of her son's good deeds. 'But that's *now*. Once they reach a position of importance, though, they change. ''The Party'' ensures they do. Don't you know it's only party unity that matters

any more, not what the voters want?' On seeing her
mother about to speak, she went on swiftly, surmising
that her parent intended leaping to the defence of her
eldest offspring once again, 'Not that that's either here
or there at the moment, except in so far as I said before—
that demonstrations appear the only way to gain their
and the general public's attention.'

Diverted, Isabel Ballard's expression turned pained.
'But a public protest, darling,' she rebuked with feeling.
'I don't want my daughter starving herself at the top of
a tree, or—or throwing herself in front of a bulldozer.'

Closing the boot of her sporty red Celica, Revel
laughed as she began descending the steps. 'Don't worry,
Mum, I wasn't really envisaging making my protest in
such a drastic form. I just want to swell the numbers,
so to speak, that's all.'

'But—but if the media's there—as they always seem
to be at these places ... And it's not as if you're exactly
unknown to them.' Her mother twisted her fingers
together agitatedly. 'Oh, dear, I do wish you had never
met this Sebastian fellow you mentioned. He sounds like
nothing but a trouble-maker to me. I can just picture
him. One of those scruffy, long-haired and bearded types
filled with fanatical revolutionary zeal to change the
world—and all while he's totally supported on welfare
provided by other people's taxes, of course!'

Revel's lips twitched. Her mother was normally a
compassionate and moderate woman, but her views regarding the kind of young man she had just described
had always been decidedly unforbearing, and well-
known.

'Yes, well, he may be filled with fanatical zeal to save
the environment, but I can assure you he's not scruffy
even though his hair may be somewhat long and he does
sport a beard. While as for being supported on welfare...'
she shrugged '...I wouldn't know. Not that I can see
what that has to do with anything in this instance, in

any event. He simply wants to put a halt to logging of our State forests before they're cut to extinction, that's all.' She took a deep breath. 'And I agree with him.'

'You?' Her mother's carefully shaped eyebrows rose. 'What do you know about forests?'

Revel pressed her lips together. 'I know what's happening to them by what I see on the TV, and what I read in the papers. I've also learnt a great deal more at the meetings I've attended. For example, did you know that the timber industry is actually running out of resources, and that the Mount Winsome State Forest—where I'm going—will be utterly destroyed within three years if logging continues at the present rate?'

Isabel Ballard looked rather doubtful. 'But surely there must be some government controls, at least, to ensure that...' She came to a halt, her demeanour abruptly changing to one of unexpected excitement. 'Did you say it was to Mount Winsome that you were going?' And when Revel nodded, 'Oh, then you absolutely must look up Hattie—Harriet—Wiley, as she was when we were the best of friends at high school in Piari. The township of Mount Winsome wasn't large enough to have a high school, so all the children from there used to come down to Piari in the bus every day, and Hattie and I became firm friends from our very first meeting, until my family moved to Brisbane when I was about seventeen.

'But you know all that last bit, of course,' she inserted dismissively, before continuing with enthusiasm, 'During the first few years I was down here we used to correspond regularly, and Hattie even came to stay with the family on a couple of occasions. Unfortunately, though, you know how it is: after a time the letters became fewer and farther between, and then other interests claim your time and attention, especially once I married and had you two children, until eventually you stop writing altogether and you lose touch completely. None the less, I just know she would love to see you and would be very disappointed if you didn't call in while you were there. So you must promise me that you'll do that—that you will look her up. You will, won't you, darling?' She gazed at her daughter cajolingly, and Revel ran a hand helplessly through her short, gamine-cut dark hair.

'Mum... I'm not going on a social visit. I'm going up there to demonstrate.' She expelled an expressive breath. 'Besides, isn't there more than a chance that she doesn't even live there any more?'

'W-e-ll, I suppose that is always a possibility,' her mother was forced to admit, albeit without much conviction. 'Although I would be very surprised if she had left. Hattie loved Mount Winsome, the peace and quiet of it, the smallness of it. Why, she even used to say Piari was too big for her, and, goodness above, that was no bustling metropolis, especially in those days.' She paused briefly before adding confidently, 'No, I'm positive you'll find her still there.'

'And if she isn't Harriet Wiley any longer? If she's married and changed her name?' Revel asked wryly.

Isabel Ballard gave a highly amused chuckle. 'Darling, everyone knows *everyone* in Mount Winsome. Even if she had changed her name a dozen times, everyone in town would still know who you were meaning... and be able to recount all those name changes with as much accuracy as Hattie herself, I don't doubt. It's that kind of a community.' Her blue eyes locked with her daughter's. 'So you will go and see her, won't you, Revel? For me?'

Revel sighed defeatedly. 'OK, just for you,' she submitted, half smiling ruefully, and kissed her mother's cheek. 'But now I must be going, otherwise it's likely to be dark by the time I arrive, and since I don't know the area...' With an explicit lift of her shoulders, she turned to leave.

'Oh, but where will you be staying, if we need to contact you, or even just to make sure you're all right?'

Isabel Ballard called after her anxiously. 'I seem to re-member there was a hotel in town. A reasonable-sized one, in fact. Like a lot of those towns, it had a much larger population last century.'

Halting her descent of the steps, Revel turned to face her parent once more. 'Well, actually, Sebastian said they would be setting up camp near the forest.'

'You mean...tents—and that sort of thing?' Her mother first looked horrified and then ironically amused at the idea. 'And *you're* going to camp? You, who've never shown the slightest desire for anything but the most comfortable of surroundings in your life before?'

Revel coloured self-consciously but still managed to claim with feigned nonchalance, 'Mmm, that's right. Sebastian says everyone just pitches in together.'

Isabel Ballard's lips compressed. '"Sebastian says, Sebastian says"... You're beginning to sound like a parrot, Revel. Don't you have any thoughts of your own any more?' she chided. 'Although I can just imagine that's precisely what *Sebastian* would say. How nice and cosy it will be for him...and all the others of his ilk!'

'Oh, Mum, it's not like that,' her daughter promptly defended a trifle impatiently. Why did her mother have to immediately believe the worst? 'It's simply a group of people with a common goal getting together to plan their tactics, that's all. Besides, I'm twenty-two years old and well able to take care of myself, in any case.'

Her mother appeared slightly more mollified, but still huffed, 'With your talk of tactics, you make it sound as if it's a battle.'

'That's what Seb...' Revel came to a somewhat sheepish halt, not even completing the man's name, let alone the sentence, on realising what she had been about to say yet again. Then, with a mischievous light sud-denly entering her turquoise eyes, 'While as for you wanting to check to see how I am—well, maybe you'd better ensure you keep tuned to the news on the TV. You never know, if they *do* have a camera crew up there, I might be able to give you a wave to let you know I'm fine.'

'*Revel*!' her mother all but shrieked, looking quite faint at the prospect. 'How could you even consider such a thing? What would your father's associates think…and Quentin's, too? Oh, dear, I do wish you had mentioned your intentions before your father left this morning. He would have known what to do, how to talk some sense into you. This dreadful Sebastian man seems to have made you lose your mind. Or at least your ability to think rationally.'

'Because Dad and Quentin would consider protecting their public images far more important than my wish to protect the forests?'

For the first time anger made itself noticeably felt in Isabel Ballard's expression. 'No! And that's not only untrue, Revel, but quite unfair as well! You should know very well that neither your father nor Quentin would put their public image before anything you truly believed in, even though, in this instance particularly, it would appear you won't be doing anything that's likely to help promote them. They would simply wish to assure themselves that you were fully aware of any possible repercussions that might possibly rebound on *you*! I mean, just for a start, people do get *arrested* at these demonstrations.'

'Although usually they're only minor offences warranting a fine,' Revel dismissed lightly. 'In any event, as I said, I wasn't planning on doing anything outlandish, anyway. Look, I honestly haven't turned into a rabid greenie overnight, I promise you. I am truly interested, though, and I just thought this demonstration might be an opportunity to involve myself in some small way, and at the same time see for myself just what is happening to our forests.' Pausing, she made a deprecatory gesture. 'I'm sorry for what I implied about Dad and Quentin. It was probably just my guilty conscience at work because I didn't mention it to them in case they did try to talk me out of it.'

'Then if you're not that committed——'

'That wasn't the reason, Mum,' came the intervening repudiation with a shake of the head. 'I just meant it wouldn't have served any purpose. All we would have done is talk round and round in circles, wasting the time of all of us.' An ironic half-laugh escaped. 'Lord, I seem to be having enough trouble convincing you of my reasons for going. I shudder to think what it would have been like trying to convince both of them. But now...I really must fly. I'll try and give you a ring in a few days to let you know how I am, OK?' Revel proposed as she continued down the last of the steps and opened her car door.

Her mother could only nod resignedly. 'Just take care of yourself, that's all.' A slight pause. 'And remember we're here if you need us.'

Slipping into the driver's seat, Revel closed the door behind her. 'I will—on both counts. And thank you,' she acknowledged with a fond smile and a wave, and, leaning forward to switch on the ignition, was soon pulling out of the driveway and heading for the Pacific Highway leading north.

Fortunately, the freeway wasn't too crowded and she was able to keep to a constant speed. Leaving first the suburbs and then the outer environs of the city behind, she was shortly passing dairy and beef cattle farms. Then, the further north she drove, sugar cane and tropical-fruit cultivation—bananas, pineapples, avocados—became more dominant, together with tracts of both native forests and plantations of exotic pines.

By the time she reached Piari it was after four, and it took another half-hour to travel the narrow, winding road that led through lush gullies containing crystal-clear creeks edged with a myriad ferns and palms before ascending between tall forests of heavily scented gums to the small plateau where Mount Winsome was situated.

It was a pretty town, with the one or two main streets it clustered around lined with shady, spreading trees, and set against a backdrop of even higher, thickly covered ranges that reached up to the cloudless sky, behind which the noticeably cooling autumn sun was now beginning to sink. But, knowing that dusk and then quickly thereafter darkness would soon be upon her, Revel didn't stop. Continuing through the town, she started looking for the haulage road that Sebastian had mentioned as leading to where the demonstrators' camp was to be located.

An hour or more and many wrong turns and dead ends later Revel could only conclude that it would be decidedly more prudent if she returned to Mount Winsome and put up at the hotel for the night—before she became totally disorientated and lost her way altogether!

Evidently the directions she had received left something to be desired, and no doubt the camp would be easier to locate in the morning, in any case, and especially after making some enquiries in town as to its whereabouts.

In the main the streets of Mount Winsome were empty on Revel's return, the only commercial buildings showing any lights being a small café-cum-takeaway and the hotel. But it was at the latter that most of the human activity appeared to be taking place, as people, either singly or in groups, and men for the most part, made their way into the bar, or else departed, presumably for home.

That it happened to be Friday night was the reason for such an unexpectedly large crowd of patrons, no doubt, deduced Revel on entering the wide hallway that led past an open doorway to the somewhat noisy bar before reaching the reception counter. At the far end a wide, ornately carved and polished staircase gave access to the upper floor.

Behind the counter, a tall, thick-set man in his middle forties was talking on the phone, his expression serious, but at Revel's approach he brought his conversation to an end swiftly and, replacing the receiver in its cradle, eyed her enquiringly with a smile lightening his features.

'Yes? Is there something I can do for you?' he asked in a friendly voice, and Revel nodded.

'I'd like a room for the night, please, if you have one.'

'Mmm, I think we can manage that for you,' he returned affably. 'Although we're close to booked out at the moment, owing to the greenies invading the place——' His mouth shaped in an expression of disgust. 'It's likely to be a case of no custom at all in the future if they get their damned way.'

Revel swallowed. 'Oh?' She suspected that now might not be the most judicious time to mention her reason for being in Mount Winsome. He might suddenly find there wasn't a room for her in the hotel, after all. As it was, she deduced that her style of dress—tailored trousers, silk blouse and neck-scarf—was the cause of his forthcoming comments. It was not the usual attire—evidently in his point of view, at least—of a likely protester.

'Yeah, they started arriving earlier in the week to make a nuisance of themselves and try to stop honest people from earning a living,' the publican continued. 'It's a pity they don't display the same conscience about funding themselves with taxpayers' money through the dole as they supposedly do about trees.' Evidently fired by the subject, he went on angrily, 'This community has existed on the timber industry for over a hundred years, but now that the greenies have suddenly discovered it we're all supposed to forget about that, including our investment in the place, and let it all just revert to wilderness—simply because that's what *they* want.'

Revel frowned. That was something that hadn't occurred to her previously. That due to its size, or lack thereof, the whole town might rely solely on the logging industry for its very existence.

'You—er—don't feel the environment needs protecting, then?' she put forward subtly with studied innocence.

His blond brows rose. 'Well, of course it does. But with protection that's based on scientific fact, not emotional humbug!'

Revel drew a deep breath. Emotional humbug, indeed!

'And those facts supplied by the logging industry, of course,' she couldn't resist inserting with an uncontrollable dryness that was, perhaps fortunately, missed by the man on the other side of the counter.

'Who else? Together with the controlling government bodies, they're in the best position to provide them. They also have the most to lose from any destruction of the forests.'

Revel considered that statement extremely debatable. But, not wishing to become further involved in the discussion—her argument was with the loggers and sawmillers, not with some indirectly implicated publican, however unfortunate it might prove to be for him—she merely spread her hands in a rueful gesture.

'Yes—well—I guess it's a sensitive issue...' She deliberately turned her attention to the registration slip he had placed on the counter to begin entering the requisite details. Then, as much in an effort to keep his thoughts on the immediate as a desire to know, enquired on handing him the completed form, 'And the dining-room is...?'

'Just down the hall there, on the right. Dinner's any time between six-thirty and nine,' he advised, reverting to his earlier amiable manner. 'Oh, and we usually have a bit of a dinner-dance on Friday and Saturday nights. They might not be up to city standards, but they provide something in the way of entertainment, for the younger ones mainly, and it could be an opportunity for you to meet some of the locals...if you feel so inclined, that is.'

Revel just nodded and smiled non-committally as she accepted the room key he passed her. In the circumstances she wasn't sure that meeting any more of the locals would be a good idea.

'Also,' the publican added, 'there's a lounge on the other side of the bar, if you'd like a drink before dinner. You'd probably prefer it in there, rather than mixing it with that rowdy lot in here.' He nodded in the direction of the bar, grinning.

Revel laughed. 'You could be right.' She bent to pick up the holdall she had brought in with her.

'Here, I'll carry that upstairs for you.' He made to move out from behind the counter, but she stopped him with a raised, demurring hand.

'No, really, there's no need. Thank you for the offer, but it's not heavy.' And, as if to prove her point, she set off for the staircase with a light and easy step.

A short time later, showered and attired in the only dress she had brought with her—a fine lemon cotton with a rounded neck and a dropped and gathered waistline, which she had teamed with a fringed black shawl—Revel made her way down to the lounge and took a table by the window.

One of the two girls behind the counter that separated the lounge from the bar provided her with her requested cocktail, and as she sipped it slowly her gaze strayed continually across the dividing counter. On the other side it seemed all talk, laughter and activity, whereas on her own only two other tables were occupied. Her fellow protesters the publican had mentioned she supposed were still otherwise engaged elsewhere.

The bar area was much larger than she had imagined, Revel noted first. Not only did it contain a number of tables and chairs, together with the usual stools spaced along its not inconsiderable length, but also a couple of snooker tables as well. And it was to one of the latter that her attention was drawn most.

There was obviously a friendly competition in progress among the four male players, and, although it might have been their amusing ribbing of each other that initially caught Revel's notice, it was one player in particular who succeeded in retaining it—and to a degree she found somewhat difficult to accept.

In his early thirties, and an inch or two over six feet, he was a striking figure of a man with his height and broad and powerful build. The short sleeves of the burgundy shirt he was wearing fitted tightly to muscular arms of a mahogany hue, fawn moleskins encasing long and evidently equally strong legs.

He had a way of moving that was lithe and effortless and very self-assured, and Revel sensed instinctively that here was a man who always knew exactly what he wanted—and possessed the will and strength of purpose to achieve it.

As if held by a magnet, her gaze lingered on his face. His tanned features were strong, attractive—exceptionally attractive. His hair was coal-black and somewhat curly, his mouth wide and sensuous, his square and determined jaw possessed of a slight cleft in its centre. He looked rugged and uncompromisingly masculine, and yet when he smiled or laughed he exuded a beguiling, heart-shaking charm that Revel found impossible to ignore. That he also had a warm, resonant voice and a lively wit she already knew from overhearing his chafing banter with his companions.

But it wasn't until she abruptly realised that her intent appraisal was being assiduously returned by a pair of humorous hazel-green eyes, their colour intensified by the longest and thickest of ebony lashes, that she felt the full and impossibly stirring force of his personality. It seemed to assail her senses, making her pulse race and her mouth feel dry as a shocking current of arousing warmth flooded through her. Without doubt he was the most formidably virile, vital and exciting male she had ever seen, she was compelled to concede.

It was so astounding and so unanticipated a discovery—here, in an out-of-the-way community like Mount Winsome, of all places!—that even as a flush mounted her cheeks at having been caught observing him so closely Revel still couldn't drag her gaze away. Not even when she frantically tried to remind herself of her growing rapport with Sebastian, or when the stranger's lazy-lidded regard continued in a lingering survey that made her quiver at the look of masculine awareness in his eyes.

There was no mistaking that he was interested and, disregarding the wisdom of her mind that insisted she was there to make a protest, not to become involved with any other man she might meet—no matter how eye-catching—she experienced an undeniable feeling of tingling pleasure on deducing that he intended approaching her.

For, after at last turning away, he immediately handed his cue to another of those present—amid much good-natured raillery—and, supplying himself with a glass of beer and another of Revel's cocktails, promptly made his way around the bar to her table.

'I thought you might care for another drink,' he said in his warm-timbred voice, setting the glass down on a coaster in front of her.

Revel dipped her head and gestured for him to join her. 'Thank you,' she acknowledged with unaccustomed throatiness. Close to, his physical presence was even more distracting than it had been from a distance. And it wasn't just because he seemed so much larger, his muscular build more powerful. Rather, it was some intangible energy, an indefinable magnetism, that sparked a response within her that she was unable to control, so that now, as he lithely took the seat offered, her senses stirred at the idea of their becoming acquainted.

'The name's Tyler Corrigan, by the way,' he introduced himself with a lazy smile that had her breath catching in her throat.

'Revel Ballard,' she reciprocated on regaining a measure of command.

'And you're staying here at the hotel?'

Revel nodded. 'Although only for tonight.' She was astonished at the unmistakable tinge of regret in her voice.

Equally unexpected—though distinctly flattering, she had to admit—was the rueful shaping of his lips that seemed to indicate that he felt the same way. 'So you're just passing through?'

Suddenly reminded of just why she was there, Revel displayed an inordinate preoccupation with taking a mouthful of her drink. 'More or less,' she evaded at last.

Once again it seemed the most circumspect course to take, she told herself reassuringly. If he was connected with the timber industry in some way, which she supposed was quite a possibility, she suspected that she didn't want to know about it at the moment. Why cause conflict unnecessarily? she excused. It was only for one evening, after all. Thoughts of Sebastian, and the fact that he would undoubtedly consider any such reasoning as tantamount to heresy, she guiltily did her best to ignore.

'That's a pity,' Tyler lamented. Then, with his head tilting to one side, and another of those slow and captivatingly sensuous smiles catching at his mouth, 'I don't suppose I could persuade you to change your mind? Over dinner perhaps—since we're both here alone?'

When he looked at her like that Revel had the feeling that it would be all too easy for him to change her mind! But, dismayed at both the thought and the idea of him realising as much—she had only just met the man, for heaven's sake!—she forced herself to concentrate on his latter comment.

'You...alone?' she bantered with a spontaneous laugh, glancing expressively in the direction of the bar. 'I was under the impression you were very much part of a group.'

'Ah, but that was before I saw you,' he admitted candidly. 'In any case, they're not intending to stay for dinner.'

'And you were?' she asked drily.

He flexed a broad shoulder, his eyes crinkling at the corners. 'Only fools and dead men don't change their plans when it's warranted.'

And he was obviously a long way from being either! A sudden disconcerting thought had Revel moistening her lips. On the other hand, he was very definitely of an age, and attractiveness, to have already formed some attachment—be married, even—and since it had always been her policy to never become involved, even for one evening, with any such men...

'Unless, of course, they had conflicting—commitments elsewhere,' she put forward speculatively as a result.

Tyler shook his head. 'No ties, no commitments—of any kind.' Taking hold of her hand, he brushed his thumb across her palm in a slow caress that sent a sensual shiver tripping down her spine. 'Except for making this evening enjoyable,' he added on a deepened note.

Revel inhaled shakily, trying to bring her suddenly rampant emotions to heel. She was shocked and not a little astounded by herself. Never in her twenty-two years had she known a man to have such a devastating effect upon her, and so rapidly, too. Instant attraction, and any other such equivalent descriptions, were terms she had always dismissed as fanciful before, but now... Now she only knew that he drew her to him with a force that she seemed unable—or uninclined, she was honest enough to allow—to resist.

'Then I guess it would be churlish of me to refuse,' she replied in as insouciant a tone as she could devise.

CHAPTER TWO

Nor did Revel experience the slightest regret concerning her decision as the evening progressed.

As a companion Tyler proved to be everything she could have wished, and it was amazing how attuned their thoughts were on a variety of subjects. They liked the same foods, the same music, the same books. They each even had a leaning towards the older, more intimate style of dancing rather than the less leisurely form of the day.

And, in view of that easy, loose-limbed stride of his, Revel wasn't at all surprised to discover that he was also an extremely good dancer. From the very first time he had led her on to the floor their steps had matched perfectly, and it was impossible for her to deny the pleasure she felt at being held in his arms, at feeling the warmth and hard, masculine strength of him as they moved to the music.

It was also during one such dance, as the hour grew much later, that Tyler returned the conversation to the subject of Revel's supposed departure from the area on the morrow. A topic she had been purposely avoiding, and diverting his attention from, all evening.

'Are you sure you have to move on in the morning?' he bent his dark head to ask in a husky murmur, his lips brushing her temple, and the ensuing tremor that assailed Revel was only partly due to his question. 'Since you said you're on holiday, what's to prevent you from staying a while longer?'

Revel swallowed. 'I—well—people are expecting me,' she hedged uncomfortably, and against all her emotions that seemed to be selfishly clamouring for her to forget any such prior arrangements.

'A phone call could inform them you'd been delayed.'

'Th-they're not on the phone.' And, in an effort to force a rational perspective, on herself at least, 'Besides, a chance meeting, no matter how—pleasurable, is really no reason to——'

'And you know, as well as I do, that that's merely an excuse,' Tyler interrupted roughly. His eyes grew dark, his voice thickening and making her heart thud against her ribs, as he went on, 'I want to see you again, Revel.' He paused, his gaze holding hers inexorably. 'And I suspect the feeling could be mutual.'

Revel bit at her lip. In all truth, she couldn't deny it, and yet...

'It's not that simple,' she pushed out on a sigh. 'I have obligations...'

'To whom?' Tyler glanced meaningfully at her ringless left hand as it rested on his broad shoulder. 'Obviously not to a fiancé.'

Revel moved her head from side to side. 'I wasn't meaning of such a personal nature,' she informed him in uneasy accents, wanting to explain, and yet reluctant to perhaps mar a very pleasant evening if she did so. That there was a strong likelihood that he would discover the truth for himself, anyway, in the days to come, she put to the back of her mind. Perhaps by then—and with considerably more distance between them—she wouldn't care what his reaction might be.

'Yet these—obligations are still of paramount importance,' Tyler essayed heavily.

All at once Revel's spirits began to rise again and her expression to lighten. The word 'obligation' had just triggered a memory—of another commitment she had made, to her mother. Originally she had planned to look up her mother's old friend on her way back to Brisbane, after the demonstration was over, but, in view of the circumstances, maybe it would be more advisable if she did so *before* joining the protest, she now told herself. After all, she had only given Sebastian an approximate date when she would be arriving, so what difference could a morning—or even a full day if it came to that— really make to her participation?

'W-e-ll, if you should happen to know the where-abouts of one Hattie—Harriet—Wiley, as she used to be when my mother knew her...' she put forward teas-ingly, her lips curving into a wide smile.

'Hattie!' Briefly Tyler couldn't have looked more sur-prised if he'd tried, and then, recovering, he gave a deep-throated chuckle, his eyes gleaming with unconcealed amusement. 'Yes, I know her. Very well, in fact. So what would you be wanting with...?' He halted abruptly, a look of sudden comprehension crossing his well-formed features. 'Of course! Ballard. I didn't make the con-nection before. So you're one of those Ballards, are you? Hattie's often spoken about her early friendship with— your mother, you said?'

Revel nodded, almost as surprised by his knowledge of the matter as he had been by her query. 'You know her *that* well?' she couldn't help but exclaim.

'Uh-huh!' Again there was that ripple of humour in his voice. 'But I'll let her do the explaining...when I take you to see her in the morning.'

From his manner Revel strongly suspected that he was keeping something from her, and in retaliation she glanced up at him provokingly through the screen of her long lashes. 'So who said I wanted an escort? Just an address should suffice.'

Tyler's arms tightened about her imperceptibly, although his expression didn't change as he continued to hold her gaze. 'Except that I wouldn't want you to get lost.'

Revel's lips quirked. '*Would* that be possible in a place the size of Mount Winsome?'

He flexed a muscular shoulder. 'Since it can become confusing for strangers once they leave the main road, if the address required isn't actually in the town itself...' he drawled with lazy insinuation.

A frustrating circumstance that Revel had already ruefully experienced, but still elected to parry chaffingly, 'Provided Hattie does actually live out of town, of course.'

Tyler dipped his head, his accompanying slow smile stealing her breath away. 'She does. About a mile, to be exact.'

Revel nodded slowly in order to give herself time to regulate her breathing. 'Then, in that case, I guess I have no choice,' she allowed, feigning a resigned sigh.

'Did you think I intended giving you one?' Tyler bent his head to query on a vibrant, laughing note, and she had no defence against the awareness that she would have been disappointed if he had.

'I hoped not,' she admitted honestly with a dimpling, reciprocating smile, and for the remainder of the dance their conversation turned to other matters.

On returning to their table they had hardly been seated for more than a minute before a young woman in her early twenties and of medium height made her way over to them with what Revel could only describe as a purposeful tread.

Dressed in softly draped, amber-toned jersey, her long, ash-blonde hair caught back with a pair of ornamental combs, her light green eyes skilfully made-up, she looked very attractive—and very watchful. That it wasn't the first time her narrowed gaze had been concentrated on Revel in particular, the younger girl was well aware, and her first instinctive and demoralising thought had been to wonder if Tyler's professed, 'No ties, no commitments', hadn't merely been a convenient line, after all. But since the woman obviously had another partner, and Tyler had displayed no sign of discomfiture, or guilt, on smiling his acknowledgement of her presence in passing while dancing, Revel had dismissed it from her thoughts. Now she waited curiously to hear what the other woman had to say.

'Tyler! Why didn't you tell me you'd be here tonight?' The blonde's opening words were an unmistakable direction rather than a question, despite being uttered in reproachful tones accompanied by a suitable pout, and irrespective that her gaze was directed towards the man in question only for the very first of those words. Thereafter her speculative glance remained unswervingly on Revel. 'You could have joined us,' she added, waving vaguely over her shoulder towards the table occupied by her partner and another couple.

In response Tyler merely shrugged and smiled wryly. 'It was a last-minute decision,' he advised briefly.

'Oh?' The young woman at last interrupted her scrutiny of Revel in order to bring her attention back to him, her carefully arched brows rising even higher in evident expectancy.

'Mmm.' This time Tyler's response was briefer still, the oblique look that he directed at Revel across the table making her lips twitch.

Not so the blonde, whose own mouth tightened slightly in patent annoyance before being relaxed determinedly into a coaxing smile. 'Well, why don't you join us, anyway?' she urged.

Tyler shook his head. 'Not tonight, thanks all the same, Briony,' he declined smoothly. 'We have quite a lot to talk about.'

'Oh?' Avid curiosity was apparent in both her voice and expression. Then, when nothing else was forthcoming—again to her obvious vexation—she swung her gaze pointedly back to Revel once more to prompt chidingly, 'Well, you could introduce me, at least.'

Tyler's mouth shaped crookedly. 'Briony Ainsworth—Revel Ballard,' he obliged her in long-suffering tones which seemed lost on the young woman as, at last having been provided with some information, all her attention was channelled towards discovering more.

'Ballard ... Ballard ... ?' she immediately proceeded to muse once the minimum of pleasantries had been exchanged. 'Your family's not from around here,' she decided finally.

'No—from Brisbane,' Revel granted, taking her cue from Tyler and keeping her answers short, although in her case for more than just that one reason.

Briony nodded thoughtfully—satisfyingly, Revel thought. 'So you won't be here long?'

Although couched as a question, it somehow had the ring of a challenge to it and, in consequence, Revel experienced a slight bristling of annoyance herself.

'I guess that depends on your interpretation of "long",' she replied with deliberate obscureness as a result.

'Meaning, you're not just passing through?'

Catching Tyler's eye, Revel couldn't suppress a smile. 'Well, not just yet, no.'

The look that passed between them evidently hadn't been missed, and momentarily Briony's eyes flashed. Then her smile was quickly back in place again. 'So what brought you to Mount Winsome in the first place?' She uttered a little laugh. 'I mean, it's not exactly known as a Mecca for tourists.' A slight pause and her glance became more penetrating. 'You're acquainted with people in the area, are you?'

'Well, not acquainted, precisely, but certainly know of,' Revel was more than willing to expand on this occasion. It was certainly preferable to giving an exact answer to that first query.

'Such as?' Briony had no hesitation in probing.

'Hattie.' It was Tyler who answered, and just as laconically as previously.

Not that the blonde allowed that to halt her questioning, despite looking somewhat taken aback by the information. As indicated by her succeeding half-frowned, half-laughed demand of Revel, 'And what connection would you have with Hattie?'

Revel shrugged. 'She and my mother used to be friends during their school days.'

Briony's expression turned openly sceptical. 'You're saying, you drove all the way up here just to see an old friend of your *mother's*?' she scoffed with a snort of disbelieving laughter.

Revel's stomach constricted. She wished the other girl would return to her own table—and her discomfiting questions along with her! The evening had been a most enjoyable one until her arrival.

'I—well—not entirely,' she parried uneasily. Briony couldn't possibly have guessed her true reason for being in Mount Winsome, could she? The thought was enough to send chills down Revel's spine. She strongly suspected that any such revelation involving Briony would not be a subdued one! With a steadying breath, she affected an unconcerned pose, leaning back in her chair, as she added protectively, 'Rather, I promised my mother I would look Hattie up because I happened to be coming this way. Apparently they'd lost contact over the years.'

Briony digested the information in contemplative silence. 'And it was through Hattie that you met Tyler?' she proceeded to assume at last, relieving Revel by her return to her original line of questioning, but niggling her again by it, all the same.

Just what business was it of the other girl's, anyway? A stab of disappointment abruptly pierced Revel. Or...could it just be her business, after all? There was certainly more than a touch of a proprietorial air about Briony where Tyler was concerned. With good reason, perhaps?

And maybe something of her doubts showed, because it was Tyler who took it upon himself to respond to that girl's last comment, and in a considerably shorter tone than anything he had used previously.

'As it happens, no. Revel hasn't even been to see Hattie as yet. But now——' beginning to rise to his feet '—the band is starting to play again, and——' a brief glance was directed towards Briony's table '—Kirk is trying to attract your attention, so if you'll excuse us...' Turning away from her, he held out his hand to Revel, the encouraging smile accompanying the action making her heart beat faster, and she forgot everything but the exciting warmth and feel of his fingers clasped about her own as she willingly placed her hand in his and allowed him to draw her to her feet and on to the dance-floor.

Left with no other choice, Briony uttered a disgruntled huff and finally made her way back to her companions.

'I'm sorry about the third degree, but don't let anything Briony might say disturb you,' Tyler recommended reassuringly as he took Revel into his arms and they began moving to the music. 'Unfortunately, her mother's the town gossip and, in this instance, it's definitely a case of "like mother, like daughter".'

Revel nodded. Then, moistening her lips and without quite looking at him, still felt compelled to venture, 'Although she did seem to—to give the impression that she somehow had the—the right to know why you were——'

'And I thought I'd already told you no one had any such rights where I was concerned,' he interrupted softly, a finger beneath her chin ensuring that she couldn't evade his gaze any longer. 'And I don't lie, Revel.'

Revel swallowed. As much because of the sudden awareness of how close their mouths were, of how little it would take to bring their lips together, as from the disquieting knowledge that, if she hadn't precisely lied to him, then she hadn't actually been completely honest either.

'Then—then...' It was all she could do to falter as she made a desperate attempt to squash her feelings of guilt—and to prevent her ungovernable imagination dwelling on the prospect of what it would be like to have him kiss her.

'Why her attitude?' Tyler finished for her. He shrugged indifferently. 'Her mother's the same. Because theirs was one of the first families in the area, I guess they like to think that that somehow gives them the right to know everything that's going on in the community, and——' his lips curved wryly '—to offer their unsolicited opinions thereon usually. That's why I prefer to answer her questions as briefly—and uninformatively— as possible.' He paused, his heavily lashed hazel-green eyes holding hers steadily. 'But if you still have doubts, then perhaps I should point out that everyone is anticipating Briony and Kirk announcing their engagement very shortly.'

Unprepared for the relieved leap of her heart, Revel caught her breath. For goodness' sake, as stimulating a companion as he might have been—and certainly the rapid thudding of her pulse in response to the impact of his warm gaze could attest to that—it was still more than a possibility that she would never see the man again after tomorrow! After all, she was only interested in him, not enamoured of him, and reacting as if she was desirous of staking a claim herself was something she was neither looking for, nor needed. Determinedly dragging her turquoise eyes from his at last, she forced a nonchalant laugh.

'My felicitations to both of them, then,' she tossed off with deliberate flippancy, and deftly proceeded to turn the conversation in another direction.

Nevertheless, as they circled the dance-floor, Revel was conscious of the other girl's eyes following them on a number of occasions, the look on Briony's face abruptly making her surmise that, near-fiancée or no, the blonde would exchange her partner for Tyler at the drop of a hat if only she was given the opportunity.

Not that she could blame the other girl entirely, Revel conceded ruefully. Tyler Corrigan really was a magnificent male specimen: all corded muscle and virile strength—and dangerously attractive in both features and manner. Momentarily she spared a thought to wonder if he was aware of Briony's feelings, but then he smiled lazily and said something to her, and all thoughts of Briony fled Revel's mind as her own suddenly flaring emotions threatened to get out of control.

It was just on twelve when the band called it a night. The majority of the other diners had already departed by then, including Briony and her companions, Revel was glad to note. She had feared that girl might have had some further disconcerting probings to make if they had all left together.

Now, as she and Tyler made their way from the dining area into the dimly lit hallway, she felt pleasantly relaxed from the wine, the food, and his company, and it showed in her sparkling eyes and wide smile as she turned to thank him.

'You'll be pleased to know you were successful,' she began in teasing accents.

'In what way?' Tyler tilted his head to one side, his eyes scanning her upturned face with leisurely proficiency before lingering on her mouth in an intimate examination that made Revel's throat tighten.

'In making the evening a most enjoyable one,' she just managed to get out huskily.

'Briony's interrogation notwithstanding?' The query might have been humorous, but there was nothing bantering in his accompanying gesture as he stroked her cheek with the back of his hand, and it was all Revel could do to nod in response.

Now his fingers moved to her nape, caressing the exposed skin sensuously and imperceptibly urging her closer. 'While you also made the evening a memorable one for me,' he advised in a voice that had both lowered and deepened in pitch.

Revel's breath became uneven, her every sense aware of the vibrantly masculine presence so very close to her. 'I'm glad,' she admitted in a throaty whisper, and doubted that she could have demurred, even if she had wanted to, when, with eyes that had grown heavy locking with hers, he caught hold of her hand and turned them in the direction of the stairs.

'I'll see you to your room,' Tyler said on a thickening note, and Revel was thankful for the opportunity to escape the curious glances from those last few stragglers still leaving the dining area.

That she was equally pleased that it also meant they weren't to part just yet she was honest enough to acknowledge. She didn't know why, but Tyler Corrigan seemed to hold a fascination for her as no other man ever had—including Sebastian.

The hallway on the upper floor was even more dimly lit than the one downstairs with just a couple of tinted wall-brackets providing sufficient light to show the way. So it was that, with neither light near Revel's room, on reaching her door they found themselves in the shadows. A circumstance that merely seemed to create a feeling of intimacy, but consequently also had Revel abruptly wondering for the first time, and not without some reservation, just what Tyler had had in mind in offering to escort her upstairs.

She didn't go in for one-night stands—she had too much self-respect to value herself so cheaply—and the idea that that was what he might be anticipating swiftly took some of the glow from her eyes. Before she could even begin to think of making her thoughts known, however, Tyler turned her towards him, his hands sliding upwards to frame her face between them.

Almost as if he could see her thought processes at work, he said softly, 'Don't worry, I wasn't expecting to be invited in.'

Conversely, along with the relief she felt, Revel suspected that the other niggling emotion she was experiencing might, disconcertingly, have been one of slight deflation. 'You weren't?'

Tyler shook his head. 'I've never considered going to bed with someone to be the most promising way of beginning a relationship.' Pausing, an enticingly rakish smile caught at his mouth. 'Although that's not to say my thoughts concerning you are of an entirely platonic nature.'

Just as hers, regarding him, weren't either? Revel acknowledged shakily. With her heart beating just a little faster, she circled her lips with the tip of her tongue.

'So what makes you think there is any chance of a relationship between us?' she queried breathlessly. 'I mean, after tomorrow——'

'There's a succession of other tomorrows,' he inserted meaningfully. 'All of which I intend to utilise to ensure there is something between us,' came the addition in resonant tones as he brushed his mouth across hers in a light and tantalising kiss that made her legs feel weak and left her wanting more. 'And if you think otherwise, then you don't know me very well,' he murmured against her receptive lips. 'But you will, I promise you. You will.'

Revel could hardly think. Her senses were scattering, her mind whirling, filled with yearnings, with warnings. It was insanity. It was untenable. It was nothing more than a passing fancy on her part, she tried to impress on herself. What about when he discovered her real reason for being in Mount Winsome? And was she looking for such an involvement, anyway? There was Sebastian to be considered, when all was said and done.

A pleasant evening with an attractive escort had been her only interest... hadn't it?

With a supreme effort she drew back a space. Away from the manly fragrance of him that enveloped her, stirring something primitive in response deep within her, and away from his sensuously teasing mouth that was making her crave far more than just those frustratingly provocative caresses.

'And—and if I said I wasn't interested in any such relationship?' she forced out raggedly.

The green in Tyler's gaze suddenly seemed more prominent as his ebony-framed eyes caught hers and held. '*Is* that what you're saying?' he countered, smoothing a thumb over her lower lip in a disturbingly sensual gesture.

Revel moved her head helplessly, unsure herself of just what she did want. 'But we only met tonight.' It was more of a plaintive accusation than a reasoned declaration.

'Last night,' he corrected huskily, lowering his mouth to hers once more. Only this time in a slow, lingering kiss that set her pulse racing and a pervasive warmth spreading throughout her body.

'Ty!' she half protested, half sighed when at last she was able, the abbreviation of his name just seeming to come of its own accord.

'Hmm... I like the way you said that,' he murmured against her heated skin as his lips grazed the side of her neck just below her ear.

Revel trembled, her thoughts fragmented, diverted. 'People don't normally shorten your name?' she found herself querying inconsequentially.

'Usually only my family and some close friends,' Tyler owned in muffled accents, punctuating his words with kisses to her throat that had her swallowing convulsively. 'And now you.'

'You...don't...mind?' she asked breathlessly, bemusedly.

'I don't object to anything about you, angel,' he returned thickly, the sobriquet making Revel's senses quiver as he drew her closer to his hard-muscled length. 'And I've been wanting to do this all night.'

Finally his mouth captured hers with all the intensity and satisfying skill that Revel could have wished, and after only a fleeting, hazy moment's reflection as to whether he would continue to find everything about her unobjectionable in the days to come she gave herself up to the sheer physical pleasure of his savouring, persuasive lips as they moved on hers.

Tyler slipped an arm around her back, moulding her pliant form to him even more tightly, his free hand cradling her head as his mouth continued its stirring possession. He felt solid, secure—exciting—and rivers of liquid fire streamed through Revel's veins.

Threading her fingers within his dark hair, she clung to him helplessly, her whole being awash in wild sensation as his tongue began to work its own magic. Slowly it played across her lips, tracing each sensitive contour, teasing them apart to taste and explore the velvety inner surface with a leisurely sensuousness that drove her to distraction.

Lost in a surge of flaring desire, it was she who increased the intimacy, the depth of the contact now, her tongue that probed and stroked and entangled erotically with the warm moistness of his. With a shuddering groan, Tyler responded swiftly. His lips sucked at hers, drew them between his teeth, his tongue invading, possessing, filling until she was shivering with delight under the intoxicating onslaught.

Revel felt as if every nerve was throbbing, on fire, her entire body racked by a fierce ache of yearning that was all the more overwhelming because of its sheer unexpectedness. That she had been attracted to him from the moment she saw him she was willing to admit, but that he could make her want him with such mind-numbing intensity, and in such an elemental, physical fashion, the very first time he kissed her, was something for which she was totally unprepared.

Yet, for all that, it seemed she had no wish for it to stop either. His mouth on hers was like a drug, addictive, depriving her of her reason so that she could no longer act, merely react. With a soft moan, she slipped her hands beneath his covering shirt, her fingers relishing the feel of the rippling muscles of his back, the firmness of his sleek, warm flesh, with a purely sensual pleasure.

Tyler's breathing became harsh and ragged, and the sound of it made Revel's senses tingle. Then it was her own breath that was coming rough and uneven when she was pressed tighter to his hard hips, and a hand smoothed its way upwards over her curving hip and waist to caress a swelling breast.

Revel quivered at the feelings his touch aroused, and the way her nipple responded to the brush of his thumb by immediately surging against the thin material confining it. All at once her clothes became an irritating obstacle that she wanted to be rid of. She wanted to feel his hands on her skin, just as her own were exploring his.

The realisation shook her so much that she took an involuntary step backwards, breaking all contact—just as an elderly couple she had earlier observed in the dining-room reached the top of the stairs and turned into the hallway.

She supposed transiently that they must have been out for a walk before turning in, and was thankful for the shadows that disguised her self-consciousness at having so nearly been caught in such an intimate embrace. She was also grateful that their sudden appearance provided her with a plausible reason for her behaviour in response to Tyler's quizzically raised brow at her abrupt action.

'We have company,' she whispered frantically when he would have drawn her back into his arms again. With his back to the stairs and the carpet muffling their footsteps, he was unaware of the couple's presence. Moreover, she felt a definite need for that slight space between them in order to, hopefully, give her time to regain at least some little control over her unbridled emotions.

Mastering his own quickened breathing far more ably than Revel seemed capable of doing, Tyler glanced over his shoulder and exchanged a few brief courtesies with the other pair before they entered their room, Revel's only contribution being a weak smile and an acknowledging nod.

'So where were we?' There was a rueful tilt to Tyler's shapely mouth on his turning back to Revel once they had the hall to themselves again.

'About to say goodnight, I think,' she put forward suggestively, huskily, with a swallow.

'Mmm, maybe it was an opportune interruption, at that,' he relieved her by averring softly, drawing a finger the length of her jawline in a disturbingly stirring gesture that threatened to wreck what little composure she had succeeded in recovering. 'I'll see you in the morning, then?'

Revel nodded, still trying to come to terms with the effect he had on her. 'About what time?' A noticeable throatiness remained in her voice.

'Early!' Tyler's voice came succinctly as he contemplated her changing expression. Then, as if unable to help himself, he caught her chin and tilted her face upwards. 'Because I find I don't want to waste a minute you're around,' he revealed on a roughly deep note, and slanted his mouth across her parted lips with persuasive hunger. 'So go to bed, angel.' His lips shaped crookedly.

'While I'm still inclined to let you.' Releasing her, he touched a finger to his temple in salute, smiling gently, and took his departure while Revel let herself into her room with a sigh that was partly confounded and partly bemused.

CHAPTER THREE

NOR were her thoughts or feelings concerning Tyler Corrigan any more settled the following morning, Revel discovered. Once again she tried to tell herself that it was only a fleeting interest that was merely being exaggerated because of her complete lack of anticipation of any such involvement occurring when she had set out for Mount Winsome. Lord, the only thing she'd expected to have on her mind had been trees!

None the less, as she awaited Tyler's arrival after breakfast, it was impossible for her to deny that there had been only one reason she had taken such pains that morning with her attire of slim-fitting designer jeans that showed off her slender form to advantage, together with an aqua top that enhanced the turquoise colour of her darkly lashed and sparkling eyes. The simple fact was that, no matter how discomposing or startling the knowledge, she wanted to attract Tyler as much as he attracted her.

So it was that when he arrived a short time later she was waiting eagerly by the reception desk, having already settled her account and deposited her bag in her car.

'You look even more delightful this morning than you did last night—if that's possible,' he complimented with a heart-shaking smile, and, tipping her head up to his, dropped a lingering kiss on to her softly parted lips. 'So, if you're ready, shall we go?'

Revel thought they'd better. Before her legs turned completely boneless! 'Shall I follow you in my car, or...?'

Tyler shook his head. 'No, mine's already outside,'—referring to the fact that her Celica was still in the parking area behind the hotel. His even white teeth shone in an engaging grin as he draped an arm loosely about her shoulders and began ushering her towards the street. 'Besides, how could I enjoy your company if we were in separate vehicles?' He executed a casual shrug. 'We can collect your car later.'

Collect her car? His choice of words brought a quizzical look to Revel's features. Surely after meeting with Hattie he would be dropping her off at her car. But, on taking her seat in the luxuriously appointed dark blue BMW parked in front of the hotel's entrance, and Tyler's beginning to speak again as he slid his long length behind the wheel, she immediately forgot all about it.

'So what do you think of our town?' he asked as they travelled down the main street where shop owners were beginning to open up in preparation for their busy Saturday-morning trading.

'Arriving late as I did yesterday, I haven't really had much of a chance to look over it, although what I have seen I've thought very pretty,' she granted, her brows suddenly lifting slightly in surprise on noting the number of police vehicles in the grounds of the police station they were just passing. 'You do appear to have a larger law-enforcement presence than I would have expected in a town this size, though.' She slanted him a bantering glance. 'Are you particularly lawless characters here in Mount Winsome?'

Tyler's brief return glance was expressive, stirring. 'Well, you certainly start a man thinking unruly thoughts,' he responded in a lazy drawl, making her colour rise. His mouth tightened a fraction. 'But they're not all permanently stationed here. Most of them are reinforcements brought in to help stop the present protesters from preventing people going about their lawful business.'

'Oh!' Revel gulped. How could she have been so unthinking as not to realise that herself? But then, when she was with Tyler, didn't it seem to put everything else out of her head? One thing that did give her a little heart, however, was the fact that his remarks had been comparatively mildly voiced. A sign that he wasn't as closely connected to the timber industry as she feared, perhaps? Except that with the sun-darkened skin of his face and corded arms, and obviously hard-muscled frame, he very definitely had a look of the outdoors about him, she was compelled to acknowledge discomfitedly, and released a sighing breath. 'That's right, the publican did mention last night that there were demonstrators in the area,' she commented at last in carefully non-committal tones.

'Mmm.' Tyler nodded succinctly in emphasis, and then flicked her a disarming smile. 'But don't let's spoil the day talking about them. There are plenty of more enjoyable subjects I would rather pursue.' An expressive pause. 'You, for one.'

Relief at leaving the topic of demonstrators behind had Revel casting him more of a provocative gaze than she would otherwise have done, and impetuously quipping, 'Meaning on a mental level, or a physical one?'

'Both!' His reply was resonantly categoric, the sheer appreciation in his accompanying look flattering, if a trifle flustering, too.

'And all in one day?' she countered with an unsteady half-laugh, deliberately reminding herself that that was all the time they would have together.

Tyler gave a negligent shrug. 'That remains to be seen, I guess.'

'Yes—well...' Revel moistened her lips with the tip of her tongue, uncertain just as to his meaning, or intent, but disconcertedly coming to suspect that it might be all too easy for him to persuade her to postpone her departure yet again. 'First things first,' she forced out on a resolutely light note. 'I just hope Miss Wiley...' She came to a halt, sending him an enquiring look. 'I know she was still Miss when she was last in contact with Mum, and I didn't think to ask before, but is that still her name now, by the way? Or has she married in the meantime?'

Tyler shook his head. 'No, she's still Miss Wiley. Not that anyone ever calls her that. She's just Hattie to everyone, and has been for as long as I can remember.'

'Well, by whichever name, I just hope she doesn't object to receiving visitors at such an early hour,' she remarked drily. It was still only twenty-past eight, after all. 'You don't think it would be better if we left it until a little later?'

'As much as I can think of any number of enjoyable ways in which I'd like to fill in the time with you——' with a wickedly implicit glance that brought an uncontrollable flush to Revel's cheeks '—unfortunately the answer is no. She's expecting us early and, I might add, she's very much looking forward to meeting you.'

Revel's eyes widened. 'You've been in touch with her already?'

'Uh-huh!' he drawled with an amused twitch of his lips.

Just as they had the night before when they'd been discussing her mother's friend, Revel was promptly reminded, and cast him a look that was half threatening, half wry.

'There's something about this that you haven't told me, isn't there?'

The return glance that Tyler spared her was all innocence. 'What makes you think that?'

'The fact that you seem to find it funny, for a start!'

His white teeth flashed in a wide smile. 'Although that could just be the result of the effect you have on me. Being with you makes me feel good,' he claimed in a slightly deeper tone, and Revel felt her pulse leap at his words.

'And—and you're digressing,' she charged jerkily.

'Not from the subject that interests me most, I can assure you,' Tyler averred, taking hold of one of her hands and lifting it to his mouth, his lips pressing sensuously against her palm before he released it again.

Now it wasn't only Revel's pulse that leapt, but her heart as well. Just what was it about him that made her so devastatingly receptive to his every word and action? she wondered dazedly. The suspicion that very shortly they could find themselves on opposing sides? That that made him somehow forbidden? She shook her head at her fancifulness as she watched the trees flash by.

They had long since left the town behind and were now travelling along one of the secondary roads that she had passed the day before. She was making him out to be unique and exciting—captivating, she thought ruefully. Whereas in actual fact... Whereas in actual fact she *did* find him to be all of those things, the singularly flustering acknowledgement emerged waywardly to set her heart pounding even more erratically.

'Except that w-we were—talking about Hattie,' she stammered finally. It was a struggle for her to remember just precisely what their original topic had been.

'You might have been. I wasn't.'

'Tyler!' she half censured, half pleaded. 'Be serious.'

'Where you're concerned, I've never been more so, believe me,' he asserted with another of those looks that turned her insides to jelly. 'Although I preferred it when you called me Ty.'

Revel slumped back in her seat, shaking her head in a lost fashion. True, she had wanted to attract him, but, having apparently done so, she was none too certain that she was at all prepared for the outcome.

'You're totally irreclaimable!' she chided with a helpless smile beginning to catch at her lips. Irresistible, too! whispered a traitorous voice silently. 'You know that, don't you?'

Tyler laughed. A warm, rich sound, so distinctly masculine. 'Mmm, that's what Hattie says,' he confided impenitently, and almost before she was aware of it he halted the car on the side of the road and turned to cup her face between his strong hands. 'Besides, it's too nice a day to be serious,' he murmured in a husky tone against the corner of her mouth. 'And that's quite apart from the fact that you have a delightful smile that makes a complete joke of all my attempts at self-control.'

Amazingly, where he was concerned, it appeared that she wasn't endowed with much restraint either, reflected Revel. All she seemed able to think of was the pleasurable fusing of their mouths the evening before, and her lips were already parting when the sensuous warmth of his mouth covered hers.

Without conscious thought she moved closer, melting against the hard, moulded muscles of him that radiated such an arousing heat. His lips moved on hers gently, savouring her willing response, tasting, seeking until she was drowsy with the sweetness of it and every extraneous thought had been erased from her mind.

And it hadn't been an aberration the night before, she promptly discovered. It was there again, that immediate and uncontrollable flaring of the senses, the electric feeling that chased through her body, making her shiver. It was as if a charge of lightning arced between them, jolting them both with its intensity. Revel felt as if the earth had suddenly fallen away beneath her, while Tyler's reaction was to draw back a space, his breath coming raggedly as they gazed into each other's eyes, and then he issued an expressive whistle between his teeth.

'I don't know about you, but I feel as if I've just been kicked by a mule,' he relayed ruefully, beginning to trace the curves of her still moist lower lip lingeringly with his finger. 'And that's something I've never experienced before.'

Revel swallowed. 'Me neither,' she just got out shakily. Even now her heart was still drumming furiously against her ribs.

'So what do you suggest we do about it?'

She knew what she'd like to do, what her every emotion was craving she do, but there were other considerations—and cold, hard reason to be taken into account as well.

'I—well—we did still only meet for the first time yesterday,' she evaded protectively. 'Also, I do still have to fulfil those—um—obligations I mentioned.' And, for extra weight, 'Once having made a promise, I don't like to break it.'

Tyler expelled a heavy breath. 'It's that important to you?'

'Yes. Yes, it is,' Revel answered quickly—before she could give herself time to decide which of the two options was beginning to hold the greatest sway with her.

With apparent idleness Tyler toyed with her hair, his head tilting to one side. 'Although you could still defer it for one more day,' he pressed with a coaxing half-smile that did little for her resolve. 'It is the weekend, when all's said and done.'

On the verge of refusing once more, Revel abruptly held her tongue as a number of questions suddenly exploded in her brain. Did loggers work over the weekend? was the first of them. Swiftly followed by the contemplation as to whether Sebastian and his group would actually be mounting a protest if there was no logging being undertaken? She bit at her lip, the silence surrounding them only seeming to magnify her quandary.

And then it came to her just how quiet it really was and instantly Revel felt her hopes start to lift. If logging had been taking place in the ranges so close to them, surely they would be able to hear it. The fact that they couldn't gave her reason to exhale happily, and to have her mouth assuming a relaxed curve. And it was only then that she fully comprehended just how much she had wanted to go along with Tyler's suggestion. It gave her pause to ponder the strength of the effect that he had so swiftly come to have on her, although only fleet-ingly, and then she dismissed it as immaterial.

'Well, I guess one more day couldn't make that much difference,' she allowed with passable demureness, and knew she had made the right decision by the way her stomach flipped over at the look that filtered into his eyes.

'Not as far as I'm concerned,' Tyler countered mean-ingfully, and kissed her again before turning back to the wheel to set the car in motion once more. As they moved off he slanted her a raffish smile. 'And don't say you haven't been warned when I tell you that, having just walked into my life, I'm not about to let you simply walk out of it again so easily.' He paused. 'And I can be exceedingly tenacious when I put my mind to it.'

With that cleft in his firm chin, even if slight, Revel didn't doubt his claim for a minute. Her lips parted. 'Ty...'

'That's better,' promptly came the whimsical approval.

'Tyler!' Her voice might have been admonishing but she couldn't control the grudging laughter in her eyes.

He made a see-sawing gesture with one hand. 'Not so good.'

Revel gave a helpless shake of her head. 'You *are* im-possible!' Her gaze became mock-threatening. 'But don't think I don't know that you're merely trying to divert my attention, because I do.'

'Successfully?' A dark brow quirked banteringly and she was unable to resist the impulse to swat him on the shoulder in retaliation.

'Yes, damn you, it appears you have,' she was forced to admit, her mouth shaping with ruefully humorous resignation.

His answering grin was boyish, and wholly without contrition. 'Never mind, we're almost there and you'll be able to console yourself with commiserations from Hattie.'

'Thank you.' It was her turn to be droll now, although that didn't, unfortunately, forestall an abruptly unnerving thought: that of just how she would fare if that relentlessness of his should ever shift from attempting to persuade her to stay to being actively directed *against* her! Swallowing convulsively, she forced out of her mind the entirely demoralising idea of just what an unyielding and intimidating adversary he would make, and with a supreme effort concentrated all her attention on her surroundings.

The houses were much fewer and farther between now. The road was also somewhat narrower as it wound up a slight hill that was quite thickly studded with tall and stately trees. At the top they came out on to a small plateau of sorts and, turning in through a wide, open gateway complete with cattle-grid, they began following the graded track that led through more open country towards the house that Revel could see in the distance, and which was nestled against the backdrop of the hills for protection from the elements at that elevation.

However, just how high they actually were hadn't really registered with Revel until they came out from among some of the trees and for the first time she was able to see the whole spectacular panorama set before them. Uninterrupted, the view stretched for miles over the coastal lowlands, forming a breathtaking tapestry of forests, farmlands, townships, meandering watercourses, and, farthest of all, the sea itself, sand-edged and sparkling in the morning sunshine.

'Oh, what a glorious outlook!' The admiring exclamation burst from her lips spontaneously. 'And Hattie lives *here*?' She shook her head in wonder.

'Uh-huh!' Tyler drawled in what she was rapidly coming to think of as his typically laconic manner.

Revel could hardly credit it. Somehow she had pictured her mother's friend in a small, flower-adorned cottage somewhere. She supposed it was the popular image one had of a single woman of her mother's age, but what she very definitely hadn't anticipated, and certainly her parent had given her no reason to, was to discover Hattie to be living in such surrounds—with a house to match. The closer they came, the more imposing the proportions of the residence seemed to become.

Set into the hillside, and constructed on three levels, it was a picture of white arches and colourful, tub-decorated flagged terraces—all with that superb view, of course. It was also enclosed by lush green lawns and flowering shrubs, while across the front of the building marched a pleasingly spaced row of majestic, gracefully fronded palm trees.

Nor were the amenities that accompanied the house any less impressive either, observed Revel as they passed them on their way around to the side of the house. Swimming-pool, spa and sauna, tennis court—only stables seemed to be missing—and it all left her just a trifle open-mouthed. Her own home, being far from a hovel, had graced the pages of a number of magazines over the years, but even so...

'Just how on earth did Hattie come by all this?' she quizzed in a disbelieving whisper, gazing up at the building after alighting. 'Did a rich relative leave her a fortune, or——' her lips twitched irrepressibly '—has she been dabbling in the drug trade?'

Tyler laughed. 'Neither.' Catching hold of her hand, he made for a side-door and, pulling the fly-screen open, stood back for her to precede him. 'Come on. You'll soon find out.'

'But we can't just barge in this way, even if she is expecting us,' Revel protested anxiously, and refraining from entering. 'We should at least go round the front and knock.'

'Don't be silly. It's all right,' he dismissed her worries negligently. Then, with the corners of his mouth turning upwards in the most delightful fashion, 'She wouldn't expect me to enter any other way.'

Revel frowned, not altogether convinced. 'Are you sure?'

In response he dropped a kiss on to the end of her slender nose. 'I told you before... I don't lie.'

Still she hesitated. 'Although I still have the feeling you've been keeping something from me.'

'Ah, now that's something else entirely,' he drawled humorously, and immediately had her eyeing him intently.

'So you admit it.'

Before he could answer—if he had been going to—there came the sound of footsteps from inside, followed by a female voice.

'So it *was* you. I thought I heard the car.' A somewhat plump woman in her early fifties with blue eyes and ginger-grey hair made an appearance in the doorway. 'And you're dear Isabel's daughter,' she continued immediately at the sight of Revel, her beaming smile of welcome altering quite dramatically her otherwise rather plain features. 'Come in, come in.' To Tyler, with a good-natured vexation born of obviously long familiarity, she uttered an admonishing, 'What were you thinking of, keeping her standing on the doorstep?'

Without waiting for an answer, though it was doubtful she expected one, she turned back to Revel again, drawing her into what was apparently a casual family room furnished with deeply cushioned wicker sofas and chairs interspersed with potted palms and ferns. 'I've been so looking forward to meeting you ever since Ty told me he'd met you in town. What are you doing in Mount Winsome? You must stay for a few days, at least! It's been so long since I've had any contact with your mother, I'm sure there must be masses of news to catch up on. I know I really should have made more of an effort over the years to get in touch with her again, but——' she shrugged philosophically '—you know how it is.'

Revel nodded, smiling, and took the chair that the older woman proffered. 'Yes, that's exactly what Mum said. That's also why she was so insistent I look you up when she discovered I was—coming this way.' She hurried on, as Hattie seated herself on a sofa opposite, before that unsettling question regarding her reason for being in the district could be raised again. 'I must say, though, that you possess a lovely home here, and the view's just magnificent.'

'Yes, it is rather nice, isn't it?' Hattie agreed. She gave a light laugh. 'Although it doesn't actually belong to me. Ellis owns it.'

Revel blinked. 'Ellis... ?'

'Mmm, Ty's father.'

Momentarily Revel looked from one to the other of them in confusion. Tyler, in the meantime, had taken the chair not far from her own. Then everything suddenly began to fall into place. Tyler's claiming to know Hattie very well, his amusement...*and* his statement that her mother's friend was still unmarried.

'Oh!' she murmured embarrassedly, flushing. 'I see.'

Tyler promptly threw back his head and laughed, earning himself a baleful glare from Revel and a banishing motion with one hand from Hattie.

'Go and get the coffee,' that woman ordered with humorous exasperation. 'It's all ready and set out in the kitchen.' She faced Revel again immediately as Tyler obediently levered his long form upright with an innate grace and, still chuckling under his breath, made his way out of the room. 'No, no, I don't think you do,' she went on to deny gently, understandingly. 'I'm Ellis's housekeeper. And Ty's, too, if it comes to that. I have been for the past—oh, twenty-six years.' Her brows lifted on seeing her listener's surprised expression. 'He didn't tell you we lived in the same house?'

'No, he conveniently left that out!' Revel relayed part wryly, part angrily, vexed with herself for having jumped to the wrong conclusion and even more vexed with Tyler for not having told her the truth. She took a deep breath. 'And I apologise for having—er—misconstrued your——'

'Oh, think no more about it,' interjected Hattie, smiling, and waving a dismissive hand. 'It was understandable in the circumstances.' Her mouth assumed an oblique tilt as she leant back in her seat. 'If the truth were known, I would have jumped at being Ellis's mistress, *de facto*, or whatever you call it these days...if he'd only asked me. He's a very attractive man...just like his son.' The matter-of-fact statement was accompanied by a subtly implicit sidelong glance that brought a self-conscious heat to her companion's face.

And for a second or two Revel could only stare at her, taken aback, and unable to believe she had heard right. Then the incongruity of the matter became too much for her and she did as Tyler had. She gave way to a helpless gurgle of laughter.

'Are you sure you and Mum were the best of friends?' she couldn't resist quizzing mirthfully. The very idea of her so-conservative mother being on close terms with this evidently down-to-earth, outspoken woman was just too unreal to imagine.

Thankfully Hattie could also see the amusing side of it and joined in the mirth. 'Mmm, Isabel always was the conforming one, while I...I was the outrageous one. I suppose it was a case of opposites attracting, but we certainly always got along famously and just seemed to complement each other. She adding a little restraint to my life, and I adding a little exuberance to hers.' She gave another laugh, a somewhat ironic one this time. 'And didn't I cause an outrage when I first moved in with Ellis and Ty all those years ago, after Gaylene died! That was Ellis's wife and Ty's mother,' she explained before expressively raising her eyes ceilingwards. 'Lord, you wouldn't believe the comments that generated. Just because Ellis and I were only in our late twenties at the time, and we only had a six-year-old boy as a chaperon...well, everyone just automatically assumed we were sharing a bed as well as the house.'

'Just as I did,' put in Revel guiltily.

Hattie shrugged unconcernedly. 'Except that, with Ty failing to inform you he also lived here, there were extenuating circumstances in your case. Anyway, none of it's either here or there any more. Over the years people have become used to my forthright ways.' Her blue eyes twinkled with humour. 'I think nowadays they'd be more astonished if I *didn't* shock them all occasionally. But enough of me,' she continued almost immediately. 'Tell me about yourself, your family. What brought you to Mount Winsome? What's Isabel up to these days?'

Revel's stomach constricted, and she immediately passed over the first question in favour of the latter. 'I—well—as usual Mum's very involved with her various charities,' she began with a nervous half-laugh. Then promptly launched into a protectively lengthy discourse on her mother's past and present activities that lasted well until lunch.

CHAPTER FOUR

DURING the afternoon Tyler showed Revel around the property and they played a light-hearted though rather one-sided game of tennis.

'Enough!' Revel ruefully called it quits after losing her third set to 'love'. It wasn't that she had been playing badly, it was just that his greater speed around the court and the sheer power in his strokes, despite his patently not trying his hardest, were just too much for her to combat. 'I know when I've met my match.'

'In tennis... or otherwise?' Tyler teased as they left the court, although there was more speculation in his expression than banter, and she met his green-flecked gaze in sudden confusion.

It was true, Revel realised in some consternation. He had begun to dominate her thoughts, her emotions. She couldn't explain why, but right from the first the way he had made her feel had been different from anything she had experienced before, their being together so exciting, intense, and—so overwhelmingly right!

But, no matter how she felt, now was hardly the time to be furthering those feelings, she reflected with black humour. For all she knew she could even at this very moment be in enemy territory, because, with Tyler displaying far more interest in talking about her than himself, she was still none the wiser as to just where he fitted into the scene at Mount Winsome. And for the time being she was more than content to leave it that way, came the shamefaced acknowledgement.

Inhaling a fortifying breath, she forced a careless laugh and replied at last over her shoulder, 'Tennis, of course,' as she deliberately moved ahead of him to return her racquet to the small cabin between the court and the pool where they were stored.

A call from Hattie, who could be seen arranging cups and plates on a casual table on the terrace, presently had them ambling back towards the house. And as they did so Revel found herself involuntarily surveying the impressive building once more.

'Have you always lived here? On this site, I mean?' she asked musingly of Tyler. Since the house evidently was of a reasonably recent vintage it seemed a logical question.

Tyler nodded, his lips curving. 'One of the benefits of having been among the original settlers of the area, I guess. We sold the old house for removal—it now graces a block in town—when it was decided to build this one.'

'But why so large?' she just had to enquire, humorously. 'You don't have any brothers or sisters, do you?' Certainly none had been mentioned to date, and since Hattie had said he'd been only six when his mother had died...

Tyler gave a negative shake of his head. 'The size was the old man's idea,' he revealed, his eyes filling with wry amusement. 'I suspect it was meant to give me notions about marrying and filling the place with a host of his grandchildren.'

'But so far you've resisted the urge.'

'There's never been any such urge...so far,' came the somehow ambiguous amendment that had Revel's breath catching in her throat.

'And—and Hattie?' she rushed on, albeit unsteadily, trying to put the moment behind her. 'How does she feel about——?'

'My marrying and having children?' A whimsical quirk arched one brow.

'That's not what I was going to say,' she protested self-consciously, her disconcertion made all the worse by the suspicion that he was well aware of it. 'I meant—about having to look after such a large house.'

'Since she also had a sizeable say in its design...' He shrugged, one of those lazy smiles that so characterised him edging across his mouth. 'Besides, Hattie likes whatever the old man likes.'

Revel stole a look at him from beneath her silky lashes. 'She didn't strike me as a woman who would be so—easily influenced,' she put forward carefully.

'You'd better believe she's not.' Tyler's return was expressively unconditional. 'Nevertheless, *that* wasn't quite what *I* was meaning on this occasion.'

Revel moistened her lips. 'So—um—you know——'

'That she's in love with my father?' He nodded. 'Naturally! As you've apparently already discovered, she's not one to hide it.'

Revel hesitated, frowning. 'Not even from your father?'

'Well, I doubt she's told him in so many words, if that's what you mean.' His lips shaped crookedly. 'Although, at a guess, I'd say that's probably what it would take to have him realising it.' He paused. 'And the fact that he'd be lost without her.'

'In other words, he——' Revel came to an abrupt halt, colouring and biting her lip. 'I'm sorry, it's none of my business.' Good grief, she'd only met the man the night before and here she was delving into personal family matters as if she'd known him for years! Why should she be interested, much less care, what went on in his family? 'It's just that...well, I suppose we all have a hankering to see happy endings,' she concluded lamely. But whether for her own justification, or his, she didn't choose to ascertain.

'Save that, in this instance, I'm not sure either of them is precisely *unhappy* with matters as they stand,' Tyler returned in ironic accents. 'While, as for its not being your concern...I've no objection to discussing my family with you.' Halting their progress for a moment, he turned her face up to his. 'I want you to get to know them. Almost as much as I want us to get to know each other,' he added on a deepening note.

Revel swallowed. 'You shouldn't be saying things like that,' she breathed faintly.

'Why not? It's how I feel.' Indifferent to whether Hattie might see them, he lowered his mouth to hers. 'And I suspect you feel exactly the same,' he murmured throatily against her all too receptive lips. 'As I said earlier, I'm not about to let you simply disappear from my life again, Revel Ballard, so you'd better get used to the idea of having me around.'

Revel's breathing quickened. Did he also suspect just how much she wanted that, too? 'Yes—but...'

'No "buts",' he vetoed softly, the expression in his eyes making her heart pound. 'Just accept and let's enjoy, hmm?'

Revel sighed. Since she seemed to have no desire to refuse, how could she oppose him? 'Are you always so relentless in getting your own way?' she asked on a ruefully resigned note.

'Only when it matters,' he averred huskily, but with just enough of a hint of buried steel in his voice to have a faint feeling of unease prickling her spine.

Oh, hell, how she hoped they never found themselves in open confrontation, she spared a moment to brood apprehensively as they continued on their way to the veranda.

However, with Hattie's cheerful and uncomplicated conversation during afternoon tea, and no further anxieties to assail her, Revel was soon forgetting all such distressing thoughts and relaxing again. In all probability she was simply worrying herself over nothing, she decided reassuringly.

The shadows were lengthening and the air turning distinctly cooler—that it was autumn definitely more noticeable in the ranges than on the coast, Revel had already discovered the evening before—when Tyler brought up the subject of her car.

'Yes, I guess I'll also have to see about checking into the hotel again...since I hadn't anticipated staying another night...' Revel declared with an expressive pause and a graphic look in Tyler's direction, which merely drew a complacent smile in response.

'Oh, but you'll stay here, of course,' Hattie broke in to insist, momentarily stopping reloading the tea-tray and looking slightly affronted that any other arrangement should even be contemplated. 'There's still so much I'd like to talk to you about.' A somewhat abashed half-laugh. 'I mean, thirty years is a lot to catch up on.' Then, with a knowing glance at the man beside her, 'And, quite apart from your staying here undoubtedly being a pleasing prospect for Ty, Ellis is interested in meeting you, too, you know.'

Revel looked taken aback. 'He is?'

Hattie nodded vigorously. 'Well, of course. With all three of us being of much the same age, he also knew your mother well in the old days. So when Ty told us this morning that you were coming today——' she raised one shoulder explicitly '—naturally he was interested.'

'Oh!' Goodness knew why, but it gave her a funny feeling to learn that Ty's father should also have been acquainted with her mother. It seemed to add a new closeness, an approval almost, to their own relationship. And all of which was quite ridiculous, and purely a fanciful throw-back to the days when communities were closer and parents had the arbitrary right of veto over their children's companions, she immediately berated. Nevertheless, since she *had* agreed to stay over another day... 'Well, if you're sure it won't inconvenience you at all...' She glanced at the older woman diffidently.

'No, no, of course not.' Hattie beamed her obvious delight. 'It will be our pleasure.' She picked up the tea-tray, preparing to return inside the house. 'In fact, I very much doubt I'll be satisfied with just *one* more day of your company. A week or so would suit me better.' She paused. 'And someone else, too, I'm sure.' A subtle sidelong glance was slanted towards Tyler.

Revel's heart, meanwhile, was beating erratically, and she could feel her breath clogging in her throat. 'I—well—that's very kind and—and generous of you, but——'

'You think about it, anyway,' urged Hattie encouragingly, cutting off her attempted demurral. 'We can talk more about it tomorrow,' she added over her shoulder as she headed into the house.

'And meanwhile we can collect your car,' proposed Tyler in satisfied accents.

Still flustered, Revel regarded him blankly for a minute or two as relief and dismay intermingled within her. The first at having a response to Hattie's invitation deferred and the latter at the knowledge that it had only been postponed, not voided. Then the word 'collect' abruptly rang a distracting bell in her mind and her gaze turned suspicious.

'Did you have all this planned?' she demanded with a shocked gasp.

Tyler's brows rose fractionally. 'To have you remain at least one extra day? You know I did.' The edges of his mouth curled engagingly. 'Well, hoped, anyway.'

Revel shook her head. 'I meant, Hattie's—extended invitation,' she elucidated tightly, not liking the thought of perhaps being manipulated.

Tyler laughed, discomfiting her by the way her senses immediately stirred in response despite her vexation. 'Angel, I'm surprised you haven't already noticed...Hattie has a very definite mind of her own. She doesn't need me, or anyone else for that matter, to tell her what action to take.' He leant across from his chair to capture one of her hands, raising it to his mouth and pressing his lips to her knuckles. 'Though that's not to say I don't fully endorse her invitation, however,' he murmured eloquently, and Revel couldn't gainsay the feeling of warmth that washed through her, dispelling all her previous doubts.

Oh, lord, she wanted to accept Hattie's invitation, to enjoy Tyler's company for longer. And for all she knew she might have been able to, but without knowing the true situation, and too nervous of the possible reaction that might ensue if she did reveal her real reason for being there...

'Ty, I can't stay longer than tomorrow,' she breathed regretfully. And, trying desperately to remind herself of the importance of what had brought her to Mount Winsome in the first place, 'I gave my word.'

'To whom?'

Revel shifted uncomfortably in her chair and surreptitiously withdrew her hand from his. 'People I know,' she temporised. Apart from Sebastian, she couldn't really have called them friends. And in truth, even where the other man was concerned, judged by the number of hours actually spent in each other's company, she'd known Tyler longer than she had Sebastian, she realised somewhat disconcertedly.

'What sort of people?' He eyed her curiously.

'Does it matter?' she fenced. 'I promised, and—and no matter what you may think, it is important to me.'

'It was also important to you apparently on Friday, today, and doubtlessly will be tomorrow, yet you still agreed to stay for those days,' he pointed out irrefutably, lazily. 'Why not longer as well?'

'Because that's as long as I can possibly put it off,' she declared, determinedly instilling some decisiveness into her tone. A self-mocking curve caught at her lips. 'That is, and continue to feel any respect for myself.' A faint shadow clouded her eyes as they lifted to his. 'Please understand.'

For a moment or two Tyler continued to hold her gaze, and she could tell he wanted to press her further, but to her relief he eventually relented with a resigned flexing of one shoulder.

'OK, angel, I'll try... for now.' The last two words and the intent they conveyed, despite the lazy smile that accompanied them, immediately had the nerves of Revel's stomach tightening again, but before she could dissent he had lithely gained his feet and was holding out a hand to her. 'In the meantime let's go and get your car.'

On their return it was Hattie who showed Revel to her room. Wide and spacious, it was decorated in shades of peach and cream. The plush carpet underfoot toned in with the patterned upholstery of the small sofa in one corner and the chair in front of the writing desk that occupied another, they in turn matching the material that covered the thick duvet on the bed, as well as the drapes at the wide sliding doors that gave on to another terrace overlooking the superb view outside.

The furniture was all of a light, gleaming maple—solid wood, not veneered, Revel didn't doubt—the fitted, louvre-doored wardrobe that filled one entire wall the same, as was the door that led into the en-suite bathroom. In concert with what she had already seen of the rest of the house, everything in the room spoke of quiet tastefulness, including the two restful water-colours that graced the walls, the peach-toned marble-based lamp on the small two-tiered table beside the bed, and the exquisitely carved camphor-wood chest at its foot.

In fact, the only item that brought a discordant note to the room was her own decidedly inelegant and slightly worse-for-wear holdall, Revel observed ruefully as she placed it on the chest at the end of the bed. Normally used to carry her gear when she played squash or tennis, it looked completely out of place in its present surroundings.

An observation that had evidently occurred to Hattie, too, she supposed on finding that woman's gaze resting on the zipped green nylon bag. Except that there was just something—speculation?—in Hattie's expression as her eyes flickered to Revel's face and then back to the bag again that abruptly had Revel's pulse racing.

Oh, hell, she knows, or at least suspects! she despaired in sudden panic, and rushed into protectively diverting speech.

'What a lovely room. Thank you.' She did her best to force some semblance of a carefree smile on to her lips. 'And that view again,' she went on swiftly to enthuse, deliberately turning towards the panoramic glass doors and hoping against hope that her nervousness wasn't apparent in her voice. 'It must be really something to wake up and look out on that scene in the mornings.'

'Provided it's not covered by an early mist, as sometimes happens in autumn and winter,' allowed Hattie with a tinge of dryness in her tone.

A nuance brought about by an awareness of her guest's attempted diversion? wondered Revel, swallowing. She didn't think she wanted to find out, and so kept her face turned to the doors.

'I guess I'll just have to keep my fingers crossed that there's none tomorrow, then,' she said in falsely bright accents, although the sentiments expressed were sincere enough.

'Yes, I suppose so,' agreed Hattie behind her. There was a pause, during which the sound of a vehicle door slamming could be heard, and then, on something remarkably like a sigh, the older woman said, 'Well, I'll leave you now to freshen up. Come down and meet Ellis when you're ready. It sounds as if he's just home from the mill.'

Revel's eyes widened. '*Mill*?' she repeated on a strangled note, shocked into spontaneously swinging back to face her mother's friend again.

Briefly Hattie regarded her in silence, her alert blue eyes taking in the almost stricken look on Revel's face even as that girl desperately attempted to camouflage it.

'Mmm, that's right,' she confirmed at last, nodding. 'Corrigan's are the loggers and sawmillers in Mount Winsome.' Her head tilted quizzically. 'Didn't you know that?'

Revel expelled a despairing breath. 'No, I didn't know that,' she owned faintly. Oh, lord, what a mess! Earlier she had only thought she might have been in enemy territory, but now she found that she was actually in the lion's den!

'And I don't suppose you'd care to tell me just why the information apparently should have such a—devastating—effect on you?' Hattie put forward flatly.

Chewing at her lower lip on seeing the older woman's gaze encompass her green holdall once more, Revel sank on to the edge of the bed in a defeated movement. 'I don't think I have to,' she speculated with a despondent wryness. 'Do I?' An apologetic glance was cast upwards.

'No, I don't suppose you do,' came the expected reply. 'I had my suspicions this morning when you evaded giving a reason for being in Mount Winsome, and then of course that horrified look when I mentioned the mill. But mainly it was the holdall.' Her mouth shaped obliquely at Revel's frowning expression. 'It wouldn't have registered with Ty. Men are like that. They think nothing of squashing their gear into a bag of that kind. But a girl—and especially one of your standing—well, she usually prefers to take a little more care with her clothes when she goes visiting, not to mention including a few more than can be crammed into one of those.' She raised her shoulders graphically. 'That is, unless they're only taking the very basics with them and they're heading into a situation where the state of their apparel isn't considered of importance. Like a demonstration of some kind, for instance.'

Revel nodded sombrely. 'I'm sorry.' A heavy swallow. 'I'll leave in the morning. Unless, of course——' she looked away discomfitedly '—you would rather I leave now.'

Hattie uttered an exasperated snort. 'And that kind of talk's just adding stupidity to misjudgement!' she rebuked, and had Revel staring at her in disbelief.

'You're surely not suggesting I stay?' she gasped.

'And why not? I was under the impression that Ty was very much part of the reason for your being here, and nothing's changed in that regard, has it?'

Revel shook her head in bemusement. 'But—but the circumstances very definitely have!' She paused, her expression turning sardonic. 'And doubtless he will, too, when he discovers exactly why I'm here.'

'Meaning, as your attitude towards him has changed since learning of his occupation?' Hattie probed intently, and, on analysing her feelings, Revel was surprised to find they hadn't altered—yet.

'Well—no...' she conceded self-consciously. 'But it's surely only a matter of time before they do—for both of us,' she went on to contend quickly, feeling almost guilty now for not immediately viewing Tyler in an entirely different light. Hadn't it only been yesterday that she had reminded herself that her argument was with the loggers and sawmillers? And he, apparently, was both! 'I mean, we'll be on opposite sides, and—and I think I'd rather leave than wait to be thrown out.' She sighed. 'In any case, how can I possibly accept their hospitality when I've come to demonstrate against them? At best it's inappropriate, at worst it's just downright hypocritical.'

'Oh, rubbish!' Hattie let her feelings be known in her own inimical manner. 'Besides, I have some say in this, too, you know. I was the one who invited you to stay, remember? And, what's more, I still wish you'd stay longer.' Her mouth shaped expressively. 'Perhaps even more so now. I wouldn't really be doing the right thing by your mother if I just allowed you to go and camp with those other protesters. Conditions are pretty primitive up there, you realise, not to mention unpleasant now that the nights are turning colder.' A knowing glance was directed towards the green holdall once more. 'And I assume that's where you were intending to go?'

Revel could only nod in affirmation.

'And Isabel didn't try to stop you?' Hattie's brows rose eloquently.

'Well—yes—she did, but——'

'You wouldn't like it, you know,' came the intervention with such conviction that it actually succeeded in stirring some first doubts within Revel.

'Well, maybe I should check into the hotel again, and drive out from there each day instead,' she declared as a result.

'That would be a better solution,' the older woman was willing enough to accede. Only to continue less encouragingly, 'Except that I suspect the hotel may be fully booked by now. Only a few minutes ago I was on the phone to a friend of mine who runs the newsagents just down from the hotel and she said the place looked full to overflowing this morning, what with all the extra police requiring accommodation, a bus-load of senior-citizen protesters—always an emotive scene on the nightly news,' she put in cynically, 'plus at least two separate TV crews she reckons she saw entering the hotel.' A pause. 'You must have seen signs of it yourself when you and Ty were in town collecting your car.'

Revel caught at her lower lip with even white teeth. She had noticed, of course, but unfortunately—or stu-

pidly—hadn't paid it much attention. As she recalled,
all her interest had been centred on her companion!

'I still can't stay here, though, at least after tonight,
Hattie,' she persisted. 'It wouldn't be right, and although
I do very much appreciate your offer the house does still
belong to Ty's father and he may not be quite so
understanding.'

'Ellis!' Hattie chuckled, her eyes twinkling. 'Love, he's
so wrapped up in his work at the mill that unless you
actually forced your way in there I very much doubt he
would even realise you *were* one of the demonstrators.'

Revel's lips parted. 'You're implying I shouldn't even
tell him that's why I'm here?' She hesitated. 'Or Ty?'

'No, not exactly.' Now it was Hattie who crossed to
the window to stare through it momentarily, and when
she turned back it was with a considering look.
'Although I would point out that it could provide you
with the perfect opportunity to indulge in something that
rarely seems utilised in conservation issues.'

'And that is?' Revel probed dubiously.

'To try communication instead of confrontation.'

Revel digested the suggestion thoughtfully. It had a
definite appeal, of course. Not least because she didn't
want to be in confrontation with Ty, was the guiltily
acknowledged suspicion. Nevertheless, if she was truly
committed to protecting the environment there were other
considerations to be taken into account, she impressed
on herself resolutely.

'Except that the time for talking has passed in this
instance,' she returned in a stronger tone, and had Hattie
uttering something like a snort in response.

'It's never too late to settle matters by talking,' that
woman asserted. 'And it would at least provide you with
a comparison against the others' claims.' Releasing a
sighing breath, she began making her way back across
the room towards the door. 'However, I'll leave that decision to you.' Abruptly her mouth curved. 'I know when

I was your age I always insisted on making my own decisions . . . for better or worse.' Her expression turned serious again. 'The only stipulation I make, no matter what eventuates, is that there will be no open conflict inside this house. That I won't tolerate. All right?'

Revel found herself swallowing involuntarily. 'You seem to have taken it for granted that I'm going to stay.'

Hattie shrugged. 'As I said, I'd be failing in my duty to your mother if I didn't ensure you did.'

'But——'

Hattie cut her off with a peremptory wave of her hand. And Hattie, she was discovering, could be very quelling when she chose.

'You're surely not telling me you would prefer to rough it out in the open?' that woman queried in obvious disbelief.

In lieu of her present so very comfortable surroundings? Who would? 'Well—no—of course not.'

'There you are, then! You're staying. I knew you'd see sense eventually.' The older woman beamed her approval, which in turn had Revel uttering a ruefully resigned sigh.

It was beginning to appear as if her mother had been right when she'd claimed that Revel didn't have a mind of her own any more.

The thought was distinctly rankling, and in consequence had her promptly proposing the condition, 'But on a day-by-day basis only, though.'

Hattie nodded. 'That sounds reasonable,' she was prepared to allow now that she had succeeded in her main aim. And, preparing to depart, 'We'll see you downstairs shortly, then, and you can meet Ellis. Don't be long.'

With the other woman's exit, Revel sank into a supine position on the bed, her mouth shaping whimsically as she stared up at the ceiling. Right at that moment she wasn't sure that she even really wanted to stay—Ty notwithstanding. She hadn't even known him for twenty-four hours so far, and yet already he was figuring in her life—and decisions—to an extent that she wasn't really ready to accept.

She *did* have a mind of her own—had always prided herself in that knowledge, in fact—and intended continuing to have one, too. And if that meant putting herself at odds with Ty...well, so be it. She would rather it didn't happen, but she had never shrunk from doing what she believed right before and she didn't intend to be swayed from doing the same now.

CHAPTER FIVE

SUNDAY was a day filled with ambivalent feelings for Revel.

Having decided that she at least owed it to Tyler to tell him herself the reason for her presence in the area, rather than him discovering it by chance or from another source, she still found herself postponing doing so.

And why? she now mused contemptuously as she sat with him on a protected, grassy ledge high on a hill over-looking Mount Winsome township, the horses they had borrowed from a neighbour to ride there contentedly cropping near by, and the late afternoon sun painting everything it touched with a golden glow. Purely be-cause she was reluctant to destroy—as it surely would—the rapport between them, the enjoyment she experi-enced in his company, the way he made her feel when he touched her, kissed her. A fine conservationist she was when she couldn't even control her feelings for a logger, of all people! she scorned.

'So what's set you scowling all of a sudden? You look as if you'd like to throttle someone.' Tyler's lazy drawl abruptly broke into her reverie, startling her with the realisation that her emotions were apparently so obvious.

'Only myself,' she quipped flippantly with an ironic half-laugh. Then, deliberately reminding herself that time was running out, hurried on with a question that had been on her mind all day. 'Doesn't it worry you, cutting down all those trees?'

'That's quite a change in subject, isn't it?' Tyler's ex-pression turned curious, and it was only with the greatest of effort that Revel was able to return his glance with anything like equanimity.

'I was just wondering,' she returned with a shrug.

'Then the answer is no, it doesn't worry me. More the opposite, most likely,' he owned matter-of-factly. 'Timber is not only necessary and useful, but its beauty gives people a great deal of pleasure as well, so I'm more inclined to see Corrigan's as providing a service that allows the public both to appreciate and utilise the unique properties of wood.' He smiled engagingly. 'Besides, it's a renewable resource, in any case.'

'Is it?'

To her disconcertion, Tyler laughed. 'You've chosen the wrong place to ask that, haven't you? There's your answer before you.' He swept a hand wide to indicate the thickly wooded ranges against which the town was set. 'We've been logging in those forests since my great-grandfather's time, yet they're still here, thriving, and——' his lips twisted expressively '—it's only some in the green movement who would have you believe otherwise.'

'Some?' Revel probed, frowning.

'Mmm, the most militant ones. Those who want *all* logging halted, no matter how it's being managed, or where it's taking place.'

Revel eyed him sidelong. Certainly neither Sebastian nor anyone else she had spoken to in his group had mentioned anything along those lines.

'Because they figure it's better to have at least *some* forest left than none at all?'

Tyler's jaw tightened the merest fraction. 'Well, that may be what some of them like to claim, but emotion-appealing allegations can never substitute for cold, hard facts—which is doubtless why none of the more responsible mainstream conservation groups are among the lot invading Mount Winsome at the moment,' he declared trenchantly. Then, with his manner relaxing again, a teasing note entered his voice. 'Or are you about to tell me that you're also one of those who want us to go back to living in caves and bark huts, and existing on berries and roots?'

'No, I couldn't imagine anything worse—or more ridiculous, quite frankly,' Revel was pleased to be able to admit honestly.

'And enough of demonstrators, anyway,' Tyler advocated lazily, subsiding full length amid the long, sun-warmed grass. He reached up a hand to cup the exposed nape of her slender neck, his thumb brushing the sensitive skin sensuously. 'They don't tally with what's on my mind.' His voice thickened. 'With you around, how could they?'

Revel quivered, her conscience at once warring with the instinctive urge of her flaring senses as she turned to stare down at him. 'Ty...' She made a helpless movement, knowing it was now or never, 'There's something you should know.' And, sucking in a bracing breath, went on determinedly before he could perhaps interrupt, 'The reason I came to Mount Winsome was to demonstrate against the logging of the forests here.' There! At last it was out in the open.

Momentarily Tyler didn't move. Then he sat up with a harsh, abrupt movement, his hand falling away from her neck as a variety of emotions crossed his face.

'You've got to be joking!' The words burst from him hoarsely, disbelief uppermost in his tone, and Revel shook her head in regret.

'No. I'm sorry. As far as it concerns you, I wish I were, but I'm not,' she averred with a sigh.

'Then why didn't you say something before? There's certainly been enough opportunities.' Anger began to surface in his voice now. 'Although maybe I should have guessed, anyway, from all your—obvious now—evasions.' He paused, a mirthless, self-mocking laugh issuing from the strong, bronzed column of his throat.

'And perhaps I would have done...if my mind hadn't been filled with thoughts of you.' He slanted her a hard-eyed gaze. 'Or was that all part of the plan? To keep me otherwise occupied while you went about gathering all the information you could for your friends?'

'No! Oh, hell, no!' Revel denied in shocked dismay. 'Ty, you can't possibly believe that.' She shook her head in repudiation. 'How could that have been my intention? I had no idea who you were when we first met.'

'Although it would have been a fair assumption that I had some connection with the timber industry, since that's always been the town's mainstay.'

'Well—yes—I thought it was a distinct possibility,' she owned reluctantly. Then went on quickly, 'And that's precisely why I never asked about your work.' She exhaled heavily, her mouth shaping obliquely. 'I wasn't certain I wanted to know.'

'You expect me to believe that?' The glance he fixed her with was openly sceptical and Revel's head lifted in response.

'Since it's the truth—yes!' She spread her hands expressively. 'What reason could I have for lying now that you know why I'm here?'

'That's a very interesting question,' he drawled sardonically. 'However, there's also that old saying about "once bitten, twice shy", and I'm not about to disregard it.'

Revel caught at her lip with even white teeth. 'You think I'd pass on any information I could discover about your logging operations?' she surmised in a mixture of disappointment and resentment.

Rising lithely to his feet, Tyler looked down at her with a dark brow arching eloquently. 'Is that so surprising?' he mocked, and started towards the horses.

For a moment or two Revel watched his tall figure despondently, and then gradually her spirits began to reassert themselves. All right, so she hadn't been as

honest as she could have been, and because of it she
could sympathise with him to some degree, but that
didn't mean all the wrong was on her side...or that every
accusation he cared to make was warranted—or
acceptable.

With that thought firmly in mind, she scrambled upright herself now and headed after him. 'Well, at least
I was honest enough to tell you myself *before* I joined
the demonstration, and not wait for you to just discover
it,' she put forward on an acrimonious note on reaching
him. 'You might at least give me credit for that.'

'In other words I should be grateful for small favours
and forget the rest, hmm?' He made a derisive sound.
'Well, no, thanks; that kind of favour I would rather do
without.' He paused before continuing in roughened
tones, and not entirely of his own volition, she suspected, 'Or don't you realise the way I was beginning to
feel about you?' For the briefest time shadows made an
appearance in his eyes. Shadows of regret and disil-
lusionment that had Revel's throat constricting, and then
they were gone, replaced by a disdainfully glinting green.
'Or is it that you simply don't care?'

'No! Of course I care,' Revel found herself involuntarily admitting in a voice suddenly thick with emotion,
and even as she damned herself for continuing to feel
the same way about him in return. Why couldn't she just
see him as one of those to whom she was opposed? Three
days ago she hadn't even known of his existence. How
could such a chance meeting, so short a time spent
together, come to have such an effect on her? But amazingly, and in spite of everything, it seemed she did
care...and heaven, how she missed that lazily captivating smile that had always been so much a part of
him—until now! Tentatively she continued in an effort
to explain, 'Our—our involvement meant something to
me, too, and, no matter what you may believe, it wasn't

my intention to deceive you. Everything just happened so quickly, that's all.'

Tyler merely flexed a broad shoulder. 'Then perhaps now would be as good a time as any to enlighten me as to just precisely why you consider there's a need to demonstrate in the first place,' he suggested, sardonically, and immediately had Revel bristling as a result.

'It's obvious, isn't it?' she countered more than a little challengingly. 'The forests are being logged out of existence.'

'You have facts and figures to prove that, of course?' Tyler eyed her askance, one corner of his mouth taking on a decidedly caustic curve.

'Well, no, not personally,' Revel was forced to grant, albeit against her inclinations. Her voice strengthened as she added immediately, 'But it's common knowledge, all the same.'

'You mean, in the same way it's common knowledge that all stockbrokers, at some time or another, engage in insider trading?'

'Dad never has!' Revel was swift to defend on an indignant note. 'In fact, Ballards have always been one of the most vocal in decrying the practice, and among the first to support any scheme that might help stamp it out.'

'Just as the State Forestry Service, in conjunction with the various timber workers' associations—and long before it became a fashionable concern, I might add— have always been the first to impose those limits necessary to ensure our forests are only logged to a sustainable degree,' countered Tyler with pointed sarcasm. He drew a long breath. 'Or do we really look that stupid to you?'

Revel frowned. 'Stupid?'

'Mmm, that after a hundred years of the Corrigans earning their living from harvesting timber, and with all the money we have invested in plant and equipment— including the modernisation of the mill only a few years back—we're likely to put paid to all that by moronically logging our own business out of existence.' There was an emphatic shake of the head. 'No, I like to think we have considerably more nous, and foresight, than that, thanks all the same. We know the forests around here...and just what amount of trees they can safely afford to yield.' A brief pause, and then, with insufferable irony, 'Just because we haven't only recently discovered the environment as the latest trendy cause doesn't mean we're not conservationists, too, you know. The difference being, we believe in rational resource-management, not slogan-shouting, banner-waving extremism.'

Irate sparks flashed in Revel's turquoise eyes. 'In other words if anyone dares to presume to oppose your operations here they're either irrational or extreme,' she sniped satirically between gritted teeth.

'When they join a group like the one that's up here at present they are,' Tyler was quick to retort on a harsh note.

'Only in *your* opinion! Because I can assure you, I don't happen to consider myself either of those, and, what's more, neither did its *supposedly* being trendy——' a term she had found particularly aggravating '—have any bearing on my coming here to demonstrate either.'

'No?' The mocking disbelief in his voice was so strong, and so goading, she had to strain with every fibre to retain control. 'So just exactly what did, then?'

'Purely a desire to ensure our native forests are preserved!'

'This on the basis of your own scientific studies on the subject, I assume?'

'No, of course not. I'm no expert in the field, as I'm sure you're well aware,' Revel allowed in testily flaring tones. She went on forcefully, 'But others are more knowledgeable, Tyler, and when I heard what they had to say I thought it was time I also made a stand. And just what do you mean by "a group like the one that's up here at present", anyway, might I ask?' she finished by demanding.

Tyler was more than willing to oblige her. 'Simply that they're a radical, breakaway lobby aligned to none of the mainstream conservation groups, and who cause nothing but unnecessary trouble wherever they go,' he elucidated with savage corrosiveness.

Revel shivered, although it wasn't only an involuntary response to his fierce tone, but also due to the gust of noticeably cooling wind that abruptly swept over the plateau, bringing with it, from across the ranges, an ominously dark cloud which blotted out the last remnants of warmth from the westering sun.

'Although I've only your word for that,' she still disputed defiantly.

'And naturally you couldn't expect the truth from a logger,' Tyler shot back immediately in sarcastically laced accents. 'However, as enthralling as this conversation may be, unless you also want a good soaking as well——' his eyes lifted skywards to scan the threatening cloud almost overhead now '—then I suggest it's time we were heading back to the house.'

Revel could only agree. Yet, simultaneously, she was also discomposingly aware that, despite their differences, she felt rather more deprived than thankful when no further words were spoken between them on their necessarily hasty return journey.

Just what manner of man was he that he could still make her regret that they were on opposing sides? she wondered ruefully.

On watching Tyler and his father preparing to depart for work early the next morning, however, it was somewhat easier for Revel to channel her thoughts and feelings into the direction that she believed they should have been proceeding all along.

With an open, dark blue parka to ward off the early morning chill, worn over a red plaid shirt and jeans, the leather belt about his lithe waist hung with a number of implements, and with heavy boots on his feet, Tyler presented an entirely different aspect from the one she had seen to date. The chainsaws, the walkie-talkies, the hard hats and ear-muffs, among other things, which she could see in the back of the utility when his father brought the vehicle round to the side of the house only added to the transformation. Now he looked the part of her opposition, she decided. That he also looked extremely capable, uncompromising, and just a little formidable, was rejected as irrelevant.

Chewing absently at her lip, Revel watched the ute out of sight from the breakfast-room window before turning back to Hattie, who had begun clearing the table.

'Where will they be working today?' she asked curiously as she helped stack the plates.

'Ellis in the mill, as usual, and Ty out checking on...' there was the barest of pauses '...the block where they're cutting,' came the reply.

It was Revel who hesitated now. 'And is that near where the demonstrators are?'

The older woman flashed her a quick glance and then shrugged. 'I really couldn't tell you. I don't know where the demonstrators will be.'

Suspecting that claim to be somewhat less than entirely truthful, because she had heard the matter being discussed when she had come downstairs on her first night there, Revel's eyes widened. 'Hattie!' The chiding exclamation was forced from her in disappointed dismay as the reason for that earlier pause suddenly became all too clear. 'You can't possibly believe I'm trying to—to pump you for information in order to pass it on, surely!' It had been bad enough having Ty accuse her of the same, but she hadn't expected it from her mother's friend as well.

'Although you are intending to go up there today.' That woman eyed her sidelong as she headed into the kitchen with a loaded tray.

'Well, yes,' Revel conceded, following her with the teapot and a smaller tray of condiments. 'But certainly not with the purpose of providing them with any information from here.' Depositing the teapot on the sink and the condiments on the bench, she grimaced. 'And that's only if I can find them in the first place. I couldn't on Friday.'

'You mean, you went looking for their camp when you first arrived?' Hattie questioned, her brows lifting, and Revel nodded. 'And couldn't locate it?' Revel shook her head now, her expression so filled with disgust that Hattie laughed. 'Then how were you planning to find it today?'

Revel averted her gaze. 'I was hoping you might— um—give me directions,' she confessed self-consciously.

Hattie released a heavy breath. 'I might have left it to you to divulge why you're here, but that doesn't mean I'm willing to aid and abet you in your cause,' she advised flatly.

Revel traced the pattern in the floor tiles with her sneakered foot. 'I know that, Hattie, and I honestly wasn't expecting you to,' she said in a sighing voice. 'It's just that...' her head lifted, her expression becoming glumly wry '...well, if my attempts on Friday were any indication, without directions from someone I could disappear along one of those many tracks up there and quite possibly never be seen again.' She chanced an audacious, cajoling look from beneath her lashes. 'And Mum, at least, would be most distressed if that happened.'

Hattie's gaze narrowed, but Revel was relieved to see that it was with humour, not censure. 'That is hitting below the belt, my girl,' she reproached in rueful accents. 'And I'm starting to feel sorry for Ty... and for more than one reason now.' She gave a resigned shake of her head. 'All right, the directions to the camp only. After that you're on your own.' A wry half-laugh. 'Although if my friend's right about the numbers in town, you'll probably only have to follow all the other vehicles heading that way this morning and you'll be led straight to it.'

Revel wasn't prepared to take the chance and a short time later, after helping finish in the kitchen, and armed with the map the older woman had drawn for her, she set about taking her departure.

'You'll be back in time for dinner, of course,' Hattie called after her as she headed across to her car, and making it more of a foregone conclusion than a question.

Revel turned back with a smile and nodded. 'For sure! It will be dark by then, and, even with your map, I've no fancy to be trying to find my way back without the aid of daylight,' she advised on an eloquent note before opening the door and lowering herself on to the sheepskin-covered seat behind the wheel.

However, even with that thick covering protecting her from the cold leather beneath, she gave an involuntary shiver. It was much colder than she had imagined it would be while still in the warmer environs near the coast, and the warmest piece of clothing she had brought with her was the brightly patterned, heavy-knit cardigan she was wearing over a lightweight sweater—which evidently wasn't enough in the ranges.

She might have to see about buying something more suitable in Mount Winsome, she decided as she headed for the road, if the leaden skies that today blanked out all trace of blue overhead—and for which the wind and the rain-laden cloud that had driven them back to the house yesterday had evidently been the forerunner—continued for any length of time.

In the end Revel found the camp site quite easily, although only as a result of Hattie's map, she was well aware. With all the twists and turns and numerous intersecting tracks, she could understand why she'd had such trouble the Friday before.

None the less, it still hadn't been all plain sailing. Due to the rain the previous day—and which was starting to fall again—plus the number of vehicles that had evidently travelled the route, the track had degenerated into a deeply rutted and pot-holed mire. A condition for which she suspected that her comparatively low-slung Celica very definitely hadn't been designed.

As a result she wasn't surprised, on eventually making it to the camp—set in a cleared area alongside the forest boundary—to find that most other vehicles there were of the four-wheel-drive variety. But, on alighting, it was the weather, not modes of transport, that again took over her thoughts as she was immediately struck by the bite in the wind which hadn't been noticeable down at the protected site of the house.

Thrusting her hands into the pockets of her cardigan, and bending her head against the wind and rain, she hurried in the direction where most of those there appeared to be congregated, hoping to find both Sebastian and perhaps some shelter as well in the lee of the small bus and a van parked close by.

Before she could even reach them, however, a figure detached itself from among them and moved towards her.

'Aren't you Revel Ballard, the daughter of Amery Ballard—of Ballard Investments?' the man whom she recognised as an interviewer for one of the city TV stations questioned, and Revel's breath caught in her throat in dismay.

She might have joked with her mother about being televised at the demonstration, but, knowing how her family would feel about it—not to mention Tyler, if he should happen to see it, she discovered herself considering, somewhat to her vexation—she really wasn't interested in making any such appearance.

'Well—yes,' she still had no option but to own, no matter how grudgingly. The man had obviously recognised her as readily as she had him.

'And you're here to protest against the environmental vandalism taking place in our forests?'

Revel couldn't prevent an inward wince. Ty, an environmental vandal? She somehow doubted that she would ever put it as extravagantly as that.

'I'm here to protest against the *logging* of State forests,' she amended with careful emphasis in consequence.

'And the rest of your family feels as you do?' he went on, beckoning urgently to someone in the crowd, and Revel was dismayed to see his cameraman and soundrecordist appear and head in their direction. 'Your brother, for instance? He's fairly involved with politics, isn't he? Is this an indication of his stand regarding the environment?'

'No, my presence here has nothing whatever to do with my brother, or anyone else in my family,' she denied in purposely crisp tones. If she wasn't careful, this could get out of hand! 'If you want their opinions, you'll have to ask them—not me. I'm representing no one but myself, in a private capacity, and if you don't mind I would rather not be interviewed or quoted on the subject, in any case.' She sent him a studiously apologetic smile to soften her words even as she began edging away.

'Oh, but surely if it means helping the protest here to succeed . . .' he persisted, following her.

Revel pressed her lips together, but, seeing the cameraman about to record now, swiftly turned towards that man, raising an arresting hand. 'No, please! I don't wish to be filmed,' she told him also, thankful that he at least acknowledged her request with a nod. Of course, whether that meant he hadn't filmed her at all she couldn't be certain. Nevertheless, without wishing to perhaps create a scene by pursuing the matter, she had little choice but to hope for the best as she returned her attention to his colleague in order to inform him, albeit somewhat more forcefully, 'I'm sorry, but I've already said all I intend to say on the subject. So now, if you will excuse me...there's someone I wish to see.' With a perfunctorily executed smile, she set off hurriedly for where she had just espied Sebastian within the crowd that was milling around and over the roadway.

'So you came, after all. That's great, just great,' he greeted her with evident satisfaction and a smile on her reaching him. Dressed in jeans and an equally sturdy denim battle jacket, his beard neatly trimmed and his hair reasonably short, his dark brown eyes bright with pleasure at seeing her, he might have looked casual, but certainly nothing like the revolutionary her mother had claimed him to be, she reflected with wry amusement. 'When you didn't arrive before the weekend, I thought your family might have pressured you into reneging on your promise.'

'And I would have thought you knew me better than that by now,' Revel replied a touch disappointedly at the implied deprecation, however unthinking. 'I was simply—detained, that's all.' A faint, uncontrollable pink mantled her cheeks at the thought of just how and by whom she had been delayed.

'Well, you're here now, anyway. That's what's important,' Sebastian dismissed the matter in gratified tones, looping an arm about her shoulders to give her an approving hug. 'And you'll be staying for the duration of the protest—at the camp?' he continued, this time in the same intensely energetic manner that she remembered.

Revel moistened her lips. 'I—well—not at the camp, actually,' she advised awkwardly, and his brows lowered in a frown.

'Then where?'

'Er—with a friend of my mother who happens to live in Mount Winsome.' It might not have been quite the whole truth, but it wasn't a lie either. But for the time being, at least, she felt that it might have been wiser, in more ways than one, to leave her connection with the Corrigans undisclosed.

'A friend who's sympathetic to our cause?' Sebastian was quick to probe, and Revel uttered a disbelieving half-laugh before she could catch herself.

'In Mount Winsome? Is that likely?' she countered in the driest of tones.

'But if this person's willing to have you there, knowing that you're demonstrating against the logging, then maybe——'

'No, there's no likelihood of her supporting us, if that's what you're getting at,' she interjected to impart. Just the idea was inconceivable, if he did but know. Her head tilted as she eyed him curiously, doubtfully. 'Although why is it apparently of such interest to you, in any event?'

Sebastian's own eyes glowed with enthusiasm. 'Because if we could get some—even one—of the locals on our side... to go on TV to say how they're also worried about the environment, that they've been a witness to the progressive and merciless destruction of the forests here...' He exhaled in satisfaction at the mere thought. 'Well, that would really add some weight to our arguments.'

Revel could well imagine it would. Yet at the same time... 'But is it really imperative that we have that extra weight?' she couldn't help but quiz. 'I mean, didn't you say at the last meeting that you already had all the necessary data for conclusive proof?'

'Well, naturally we do,' came the rapid, if a trifle scornful affirmation. 'Not that we really need anything like that, in any case. You only have to look around you to see what damage is being done.'

A statement that promptly had Revel recollecting Tyler suggesting she do the same thing—only as proof that the forest *wasn't* being damaged! And she had to admit that, from what she had seen to date, it looked quite healthy and—forested to her eyes. Of course, she was far from an authority on the subject, as she had admitted to Tyler, and she might have been missing the finer points, she had to concede.

'Besides, apart from anything else, it's the principle of the thing,' she suddenly realised that Sebastian was continuing. 'They shouldn't be logging State forests.'

'Because they're the only large areas of native timber remaining?'

'That, and the timber industry's attitude of "make the big bucks today and we'll worry about the result tomorrow",' he retorted in righteous indignation. 'They're wantonly destroying whole eco-systems, among other things, and ensuring our grandchildren will never experience the wonder of gazing at a forest giant—a tree that's been allowed to reach full maturity as nature intended it should.'

'I see,' Revel acknowledged thoughtfully. Once again, as he stated it, there definitely was cause for concern, and action—exactly as she had previously believed—but just for her own enlightenment, if no other reason, she still felt compelled to query, 'But surely there are *some* controls. I mean, doesn't the Forestry Service——?'

'Them! They're hand-in-glove with the timber industry!' he cut her short to declare trenchantly. 'Their documents are biased, and their theory of sustainable yield nothing but a myth!'

Taken aback a little by his vehemence, and his inclusion of the Forestry Service in his denunciations, Revel was silent for a moment or two. Then, before she had

a chance to say anything further, an excited and urgent
call came from up the road.

'There's a vehicle coming! There's a vehicle coming!'

Whereupon everyone, and especially Sebastian, who
hurried Revel along with him, rushed to form a human
barrier across the dirt track.

'Link arms! Link arms, everyone!' the cry went up,
and whether she wanted to be or not Revel abruptly
found herself imprisoned between Sebastian on one side
and a rather roughly dressed young woman with a child
of about three years hanging on to her legs on the other.

It was only then, when a number of uniformed police
came to stand on the sidelines, that Revel noticed the
two police vehicles parked behind the bus and van she
had observed earlier, and she couldn't help wondering,
a trace apprehensively, just what the outcome of the apparently approaching confrontation was likely to be.

However, when it became obvious that it was only a
privately owned vehicle containing one person, and a
female at that—instead of the logging equipment the
demonstrators had evidently been anticipating, and
hoping for—the human chain disgruntledly parted to
allow the vehicle through. As they did so Revel got a
glimpse of the driver, and promptly grimaced ruefully
on recognising none other than Briony Ainsworth behind
the wheel.

That the other girl had also noticed Revel was apparent by the way her expression altered from one of
utter scorn, as she viewed the protesters, to one of
smirking satisfaction and triumph as her gaze collided
briefly with the younger girl's before she continued on
her way.

CHAPTER SIX

WELL, at least she could be grateful that she had already informed Tyler herself why she was in Mount Winsome, Revel mused wryly as she watched Briony's vehicle disappear from view.

Not for one minute did she suppose that it wasn't to Tyler that Briony was at that very moment on her way to regale him with her discovery—together with heaven alone knew what embellishments she could add, as long as they put Revel in the worst possible light in Tyler's eyes. Although just how much worse she could look Revel wasn't too sure. Certainly the atmosphere between them had been strained, to say the least, since the previous afternoon.

Meanwhile a number of the protesters around her were beginning to show definite signs of frustration and annoyance at the lack of any activity to oppose.

'It's beginning to look as if the bastards have made a switch and they're not logging Block Six today, after all!' complained one.

'Or else knowing we're blockading the road has put a halt to it altogether for the day,' proposed someone else on a rising note of jubilation.

Knowing from what Hattie had said that that certainly wasn't the case, Revel swallowed, and tried not to look as guilty as she felt by keeping silent. But, as she had intimated to her mother's friend, although she opposed the logging, she still couldn't, in all conscience, pass on any information she happened to glean in the Corrigan household. That would be just too much of an abuse of their hospitality, and besides, if she hadn't been taking part in the demonstration the protesters would have had to come by their information from some other source, in any case.

'Yes, well, maybe, and maybe not,' Sebastian responded to the last suggestion with a speculative frown. 'But there's one sure way to find out.' His voice sharpened with decisiveness. 'If they're not coming to us, we'll go looking for them! So come on, most of you, into the vehicles. You, you, and you——' indicating three of the other men '—and some of the others can stay here just in case they do come this way later,' he ordered, and received nods of acquiescence in acknowledgement. 'Right, let's go!' He turned for the four-wheel-drives together with the rest of them, and once again ushering Revel along with him.

Grateful at the thought of some protection, if only for a while, from the chilling rain and wind squalls that had increasingly been assailing them, Revel accompanied him willingly. Her hair was already plastered to her head like a sleek cap, her cardigan and jeans uncomfortably damp, and her trainers generously coated with mud.

That most of the others gave the appearance of being either unaware or unaffected by the inclement conditions, she found surprising, to say the least. Or perhaps it was simply that they were too committed to their cause to acknowledge such trifles, she mused abashedly as they set off with another two filled vehicles following in their tracks, as well as the station wagon carrying the TV crew, and with one of the police cars bringing up the rear.

Just exactly where they went, Revel had no idea. She only knew that by the end of the day they seemed to have travelled along every track and trail there was. And all of them unsuccessfully. Granted, they had come across areas where logging had been carried out, but of where felling *was* actually taking place they hadn't managed to discover by so much as a sight or a sound.

'We didn't even see a single piece of machinery!' griped one of the vehicle's occupants in disgust on being asked how things had gone when they at last rejoined those left at the camp. 'If we'd at least found some of their equipment, we could have slowed them down a bit. It wouldn't have been another day wasted then.'

Alighting herself, Revel eyed the speaker curiously. 'Slowed them down? In what way?'

The man's return gaze was askance, as if she wasn't too bright. 'Sand in the fuel tank, of course,' he elucidated with obvious satisfaction at the thought. 'That puts them out of action for a while.'

Revel's eyes widened, and then narrowed as her brows lowered in a dubious frown. She had read of such occurrences at other demonstrations, but had never expected to hear it suggested at this one.

'But isn't that merely wilful damage of private property?' she couldn't help but demur in consequence.

'And what about their wilful damage of *public* property?' he immediately rounded on her with an irate snort, taking her aback with his sudden virulence. 'If they don't like it, they know how to stop it. Halt logging the forests!'

'In other words, either voluntarily take expensive equipment out of use, or else have it *put* out of action,' she returned on an uncontrollably sardonic note, her own feelings beginning to flare in response to his tone and attitude. 'That's not exactly much of a choice.' She paused. 'Nor likely to help them see your viewpoint, I might add.'

'Oh, they'll see it all right, when there's too many protesters here for them to ignore,' came the sneering retort. 'They'll have to stop their vandalism then, and leave the forests to nature, as they were meant to be.'

'Although it is acceptable for you to indulge in vandalism in order to achieve that aim,' it was impossible for Revel not to deride. She didn't doubt her desire to protect the forests was equally strong as his, but there was no way she could condone such means justifying the end.

'You fight fire with fire,' he dismissed carelessly, shrugging. Then, with his expression assuming a suspicious cast, 'So just whose side are you on, in any case, that you're so protective on their behalf?'

Revel's chin lifted, both in denial of his implication, and support of her own principles. 'I'm on the side of the forests ... but not at the cost of becoming wantonly destructive myself!' she retorted in sarcastically pointed accents.

'Yeah, well, fortunately for the environment, some of us are prepared to do more than just pay lip-service to our ideals.' His derogatory survey of her person alone was sufficient to have her temperature rising.

'And so am I!' she defended furiously. 'If I weren't, I wouldn't be here! But that doesn't mean——'

'Hey, hey! Come on, cut it out, you two,' she was checked by Sebastian's sudden and coaxing exhortation. 'Divided, we fall, remember? The most important thing is our common goal, not the different methods we would each choose to achieve it.' He expelled an expressive breath. 'It's been a long and frustrating day—not helped by the weather——' a graphic glance was directed skywards into the once more steadily failing rain '—and we're all probably a bit tense as a result. But I'm determined tomorrow's going to go *our* way.' With a reassuring smile, he put an arm around Revel's shoulders and gave the other man an encouraging slap on the back. 'So let's have no more disharmony, hmm? Instead we should already be planning our tactics with the others. We might not have located where they were felling today, but they can't elude us for ever, and *then* it will be a different story entirely!'

It was just on dusk by the time Revel was finally able to get away from the meeting. Mindful of her assurance

to Hattie that she would be back before dark, and not
wanting to worry that woman unduly, she resisted all
Sebastian's entreaties that she remain longer, or even stay
overnight.

'And don't pay any attention to what Marvin was
saying earlier,' Sebastian adjured as he saw her to her
car. 'He gets a bit carried away at times, but he's harmless
enough. You know the type. All talk, no action.'

Revel wasn't so certain. The man had definitely given
her the impression that he would have acted if given the
chance. 'Although they are tactics that have been used
by some demonstrators,' she reflected doubtfully.

'Well—yes. Unfortunately some have evidently felt
they've been forced to utilise such methods in order to
get their message across.'

'But you don't support such tactics?' Revel eyed him
anxiously.

Sebastian laughed. 'We've no need to. So stop looking
so worried,' he chided with a smile, tapping her under
the chin. 'There are other ways of pressuring these people
into doing what's right.'

Acceptable ways, contemplated Revel, relieved, her
expression clearing. 'I'm glad,' she told him with an
answering smile. 'I wouldn't have wanted to be involved
in anything like that.'

'No, I knew you wouldn't,' he agreed. And, tilting her
face up to his, 'But are you positive you have to go back
tonight? I'd really like it if you stayed.'

Revel moved restively, guiltily. Far from concen-
trating on him, her predominant thought at that moment
was of a steaming-hot shower to dispel the chill that
seemed to have seeped clear through to her bones. Her
clothes by now were wet through to the skin, she was
sure, and just the idea of remaining in them any longer
than she absolutely had to was enough to have her
shaking her head in rejection.

'I'm sorry, but I really can't,' she declared contritely. 'I'm expected back—and before dark, too.' A somewhat dismayed look about her showed what little light there was to be fading rapidly now.

'Well, if you must.' Sebastian accepted her decision with a regretful sigh. 'Just take care going down that track, that's all. Your car's not really meant for this type of terrain.'

'You don't have to tell me that.' Revel's return was eloquent with feeling. 'It wasn't a particularly comfortable or comforting ride I had getting up here this morning, I can tell you.'

'Then perhaps I'd better come down and collect you each morning.'

'Oh, no, I wouldn't want to put you to all that trouble,' Revel immediately vetoed in something of a panic at the thought of him arriving at the Corrigans'. She continued hurriedly, 'Besides, there's really no necessity. I did still manage this morning, and can see no reason why I shouldn't do the same in future as well. I'm sure there must be far more important matters requiring your attention here than to waste your time collecting me.'

A claim he was hardly in a position to deny. 'Well, if you're certain...'

'She's never let me down yet,' asserted Revel quickly, giving a meaningful pat to the roof of the Celica. 'But now I absolutely must be going.' She opened the door, preparing to slide inside. 'So I'll see you in the morning.'

'Bright and early,' Sebastian averred and, bending his head, dropped a brief kiss on her rain-damp cheek.

It was the first time he had sought to advance their friendship to a more personal level, although it wasn't entirely unexpected. What Revel hadn't anticipated, though, was the fact that the only effect it had on her was the registration that his beard scratched. Apart from that—nothing. She found it disconcerting at best when by comparison it appeared that Tyler only had to *look* at her in a certain fashion to have her every sense responding.

The realisation had her still mulling it over in her mind even after she had taken her departure from Sebastian and begun the trip down to the plateau below. And was the chief reason, she didn't doubt, for her becoming hopelessly lost on the way!

That the track she had somehow managed to get herself on finished in a dead end certainly didn't improve her humour, although just what she discovered at that dead end did provide her with a moment's involuntary ironic amusement.

Good lord, she had just located the heavy logging machinery they had been searching for all day! No wonder they hadn't been able to find it. They must have been miles away in the opposite direction.

But worse was still to come, had she but known it, for, in turning to leave, she couldn't see the mire created by that equipment, with the result that, in reversing, her car became inextricably bogged.

Oh, hell, that's all I need! Revel promptly despaired, switching off the engine. Now what was she supposed to do? Eventually she settled on attempting to make it to the main road on foot, from where she could hopefully hitch a lift—it surely couldn't be far away now— and trust the exertion to keep the cold at bay.

She was thankful that the rain had eased to a light drizzle, at least, although she was soon to discover, with a grimace and an uncontrollable shiver, that, if anything, the wind had intensified. It swept down from the top of the range in icy blasts that made the trees sway, and cut through her damp clothing as if it were nonexistent.

She hadn't even gone half a mile before her hands and face, especially, felt frozen, her teeth beginning to chatter, and she was on the verge of turning back—even a night in a cold car had to be better than this!—when from out of the blackness a pair of headlights suddenly appeared and her heart leapt with thankfulness as she waited impatiently for the vehicle to reach her.

That it turned out to be the Corrigans' ute, and Tyler who literally flung himself out from behind the wheel immediately the vehicle halted beside her, had a good deal of her relief dissipating, nevertheless.

Dressed in the same clothes as when she had last seen him, he seemed to loom over her like some dark, avenging force, and she didn't need to be told that he was considerably less pleased to see her than she was to see him. She might not have been able to see the grimness of his expression—he had his back to the headlights— but it was unmistakably there in the glitter of his eyes, the hard set of his shoulders, and the barely controlled violence in his movements.

'Just what the hell are you doing down here?' he immediately demanded in a grating voice full of suspicion. And, without giving her a chance to answer, 'Where are the others?' His eyes narrowed as he peered past her in the direction from which she had just come.

'Th-there are n-no others,' Revel stammered between her ungovernably chattering teeth, and trying desperately to overcome the mixed feelings of regret and vexation that were swamping her. Of course, she had expected his demeanour towards her to change on discovering her reason for being at Mount Winsome, but she really hadn't been prepared for the empty feeling inside which was now besetting her at that estrangement. It seemed that her senses, at least, weren't quite as prepared to accept him as the opposition as her mind felt they should. 'Th-the only reason I'm h-here is because I g-got lost on my way back t-to the main road.'

'You don't mind if I check?' His sarcastic tone was as disheartening as his evident lack of belief. 'Or am I supposed to just accept that you're walking around in the dark, in this weather, for the sheer fun of it?'

Revel's lips compressed. 'M-my car became b-bogged at the dead end back th-there,' she explained with an embarrassed grimace.

'Where our equipment is?' Tyler promptly rasped on a taut note, and she nodded. 'How incredibly convenient! But then you'll have no objections to accompanying me down there, I'm sure...just to make certain.'

Revel shook her head. Anything, if it meant getting out of the biting wind! 'Y-you might even be able to p-pull my car f-free,' she suggested hopefully, having noticed the winch on the front of his own vehicle.

'*If* it needs it...and *if* I feel so inclined,' Tyler qualified callously. He moved slightly, and she saw a derisively mocking curve shape his mouth as the headlights illuminated one side of his face. 'And you don't have to quaver. I may feel like killing you for being such a deceiving little bitch, but I'll try and refrain from doing so...if only for Hattie's sake!'

Revel swallowed painfully, knowing that she couldn't, in all honesty, altogether deny the derogatory description. 'My v-voice is shaking because I'm so c-cold,' she still defended what she could, wrapping her arms about herself in the faint hope of generating some extra body heat as another compulsive shiver shook her. 'M-my clothes have been w-wet for most of the d-day, and——' She broke off in sudden confusion as Tyler abruptly raised a hand to feel the shoulder of her cardigan and then laid his knuckles against the chilled skin of her cheek.

'Bloody hell!' The roughly voiced exclamation seemed dragged from him in shock. 'You're half frozen! In the name of all that's holy, why on earth didn't you wear something warmer...and waterproof? You must have seen what the weather was going to be like this morning.'

Revel lifted a deprecating shoulder. 'Th-these are the warmest c-clothes I brought with me,' she advised with yet another uncontrollable chatter of her teeth, and Tyler uttered a graphic expletive.

'Then for crying out loud, get in the ute, will you?' It wasn't a question but very definitely a command as, with an inflexible grip on her upper arm, he hustled her around to the passenger door and, upon opening it, literally thrust her inside. 'Before you catch bloody pneumonia, and give me even more reason to regret your coming by expiring on our damn doorstep!' Slamming the door shut after her, he stalked back around the vehicle to take his own seat.

Warmed both physically and emotionally by the fact that he switched the heater to high as soon as the engine rumbled to life and they began moving, Revel turned to him impulsively for confirmation of her earlier deduction.

'Briony also told you—about seeing me today, I suppose?' she sounded flatly.

Tyler nodded sharply without looking at her, his hands seeming to tighten marginally on the wheel. 'And how close you appeared to be with Renwick.'

Revel's eyes widened. 'Close! We had our arms linked, that's all!' she expostulated, albeit not without a tinge of guilt.

'Which is what I thought initially might have been the case. Undoubtedly you'll find it amusing to learn that I supposed it was merely another of her attempts to sow dissension—as she often does when she's been deprived of information she considers her due.' Now he did look at Revel, with an icily raking green gaze. 'But then the news on the TV confirmed her claim by catching the pair of you on at least two occasions with his arm securely around you.'

Revel chewed at her lip despairingly. Oh, damn, why did it matter what he thought? Wasn't Sebastian's friendship enough? She had known him first, after all. But it seemed that no matter what attempts at rationalisation she made the insidious attraction Tyler held for her refused to be dispelled and had her reaching out a tentative hand.

'Ty...it's not what it might seem.'

'No, of course not. Just as your being here now isn't as it might seem either, I suppose?' he scorned, unmoved.

Revel's lips parted as realisation dawned. 'You think I'm here because I was searching for your equipment?' she gasped.

They had reached the end of the track now and, stopping the vehicle, Tyler extracted a torch from the glove-compartment before looking at her over his shoulder, his expression grim, as he prepared to alight.

'In view of Renwick's aims, is that so unlikely?' he derided, and thrust open his door.

Since nothing could have been further from the truth, Revel eyed his tall figure with something of a glower as it disappeared into the blackness. It was an accusation which she would take great pleasure and satisfaction from seeing disproved, she consoled herself. With this thought in mind, she left the ute herself now—if grudgingly, in view of the fact that the temporary respite from the rain was over and it had once again started to pelt down as heavily as at any time earlier in the day. A circumstance that had her mouth pulling into a disgruntled moue as she headed for the moving torchlight.

'Well, do you believe me now?' she began on a faintly gibing note immediately she was within speaking distance. 'I told you no one else was here.' And, on noting that he wasn't only checking the surrounds, but also the equipment itself, 'Nor has anyone *been* here to tamper with your machinery either.'

'*Yet*!' The qualification was ground out with savage explicitness. 'And if that's all you volunteered for another icy soaking in order to say, then I suggest you get back in the ute right now...before you freeze your damned fool self to death altogether!'

With a hand in the small of her back, he began propelling Revel back the way she had come, and, despite a niggling indignation at his arbitrary action, Revel offered no protest. Her teeth *were* beginning to chatter again, and the shelter and warmth provided by his vehicle had been welcome.

None the less, when they passed her Celica with merely a cursory glance on Tyler's part, she felt compelled to object, 'B-but what about my car? You really don't intend to help me get it out?' She couldn't keep the hurt from her tone or her expression as she looked back at him.

'Not tonight, in this weather,' he had no compunction in informing her summarily, and already opening the ute's passenger door. 'It can wait till morning. The rain should be gone by then.'

'Oh, but I've arranged to meet——'

'Your mates? So you can tell them the happy result of your search?' he promptly charged disparagingly. 'Well, I'm afraid they're just going to have to be disappointed on this occasion.'

Revel drew a resentful breath. 'Except that I wasn't searching in the first place!' she flared. 'As I told you, the only reason I'm here is because I took the wrong damn turning somewhere back there.' She flung out a hand towards the high side of the range.

Briefly their glances continued to hold, cynical versus reproachful, and then Tyler abruptly shook his head, breaking the contact, and scrubbed a hand through his hair that Revel suddenly realised was now as saturated as her own.

'Well, whatever the reason, I rather think your need for a hot shower and some dry clothing is somewhat more pressing at the moment than any such discussion,' he put forward on a gruff note. 'So if you'll get in the car...'

Revel didn't immediately move. Instead her gaze flickered back to his as her breathing constricted. If he could show concern for her well-being, he couldn't be *totally* alienated, could he?

'Ty——'

'Just get in the car, Revel, for heaven's sake!' Tyler cut her off roughly, his voice sharpening once more, and, affecting an indifferent shrug, she did as directed.

'My car will be all right there, won't it?' she still felt constrained to ask in an anxious voice when he took the seat beside her.

Leaning across to replace the torch, he fixed her with a taunting look. 'Why? Worried that when you return it might be to find that someone's indulged in a little retaliation—by slashing *your* tyres and wrecking *your* fuel system?' he countered caustically, straightening.

Revel swallowed and glanced at him in dismay. Actually, that hadn't occurred to her, but now that he had raised the matter...

'And is that likely to happen?' she probed tightly, suddenly unable to help wondering if that hadn't been the real reason for his proposing to leave her car where it was, but at the same time struggling not to let him see how painful the idea was to her.

For a moment Tyler didn't answer. Then, with a sardonic twist catching at his lips, he seemed to relent and relieved her anxiety by advising, 'Oh, don't worry. That's not our way. We leave that kind of behaviour to your *caring* mates.' Switching on the engine, he reversed— without mishap on his part—and began accelerating up the track.

'They're not my mates, only—associates of a sort, I suppose,' she contradicted quietly at length.

'Or accomplices,' he was quick to amend on a scathing note.

Refusing to be drawn, Revel continued as if he hadn't spoken. 'And, although you may not believe it, sabotaging your, or anyone else's equipment, for that matter, is not something that I find acceptable. Far from it, in fact. As I made plain to one of the men at the camp this afternoon.' Her expression took on an ironic cast. 'And for which effort, I might add, I was accused of supporting the loggers!'

The barest quirk touched Tyler's lips and then swiftly disappeared. 'Although your—professed opposition to their practices still isn't sufficient to have you reconsidering your association with them, evidently,' he scorned.

Revel's chin angled higher. 'Since it was only one man who even voiced such a suggestion, why should it? And particularly when your own actions are equally reprehensible! Even to the extent, as I learned today, that you're carrying out panic-logging by felling trees not yet marked by the Forestry Service because you're scared our protest will stop the logging altogether,' she denounced irefully.

'The hell we're felling unmarked trees!' Tyler's blazing repudiation was even more furiously voiced. 'And I can, and will, prove it to you. So forget any other arrangements you might have made, sweetheart, because you have just secured yourself an appointment to check the yard at the mill tomorrow. And if you can find *one* unmarked log anywhere on that site I'll guarantee to shut down the mill voluntarily!'

His vehemence was persuasive, Revel had to concede. His high-handedness regarding her arrangements was something else again, though. 'Except that I've not the slightest wish to see over your mill site,' she snubbed as a result.

The line of Tyler's jaw hardened. 'Because you prefer to deal in unfounded allegations that appeal to the emotions rather than in facts? Because you're too frightened you might actually discover the truth of the matter?' he derided, slanting her a contemptuous gaze that had her colour rising unbidden.

'No, of course not!' she defended vexedly.

'Then prove it! By inspecting the mill tomorrow.'

'I'm expected elsewhere tomorrow!' she heaved.

'Where you'll doubtlessly demonstrate—for the benefit of the TV cameras, naturally—against claimed practices you refuse to investigate for veracity!' he slated in a tone of utter disgust.

'I've only your word for it that they are unfounded allegations,' she countered protectively, bristling.

'And whose word that they're not?' A dark brow was arched sarcastically. 'Some cloud-cuckoo-land inhabitant from your rent-a-cause mob whose major interest is in closing down *all* industry... under the guise of conserving the environment?'

Revel pressed her lips together. 'And that's just typical of the remarks made by people like you concerning the green movement,' she retorted tartly.

'No, not all the green movement,' Tyler was swift to contradict on a terse note. 'Just those militant fringe groups who seem to consider themselves above the law, and that any means whatsoever is justified in achieving their aims.'

Meaning, once again, by damaging their equipment, Revel deduced, and was pleased to be able to rebut herself now, 'Which just proves how wrong you are in this instance, because Sebastian told me himself there was no need to sabotage your machinery due to there being other ways of bringing pressure to bear on you.'

'Like hammering nails and steel spikes into the trees, for example?' He flashed her a narrowed glance. 'So is that what you've been doing all day?'

Revel returned his gaze blankly. 'Hammering nails and spikes into the trees? Whatever for?'

Momentarily Tyler didn't answer, then he gave a disbelieving shake of his head and recommended sardonically, 'Do yourself a favour, sweetheart, and go back to Brisbane. You're getting yourself into something you apparently know very little about.'

'And that's for me to decide, not you,' she rejoined tartly, bridling. 'So, instead of being so damned patronising, why not try explaining?'

'Because I would have thought it was obvious,' he wasn't averse to biting back. 'Nails and such in the trees can wreak havoc. To both the feller, if he should happen to hit them with his chainsaw, and to anyone who happens to get in the way when the log's processed at the mill, if the high-speed blades connect with them and shatter.'

Appalled at the idea of either circumstance, Revel abruptly found one particular thought surging to the front of her mind.

'And do you work in the mill, or are you a feller?' she queried with uncontrollable apprehension.

For a fleeting moment Tyler surveyed her intently, and then he shrugged and returned his attention to the road. They were almost down on to the plateau now.

'I do my share of felling on occasion, although I mostly just co-ordinate it and oversee the equipment,' he relayed flatly.

Revel nodded and released an unconsciously held breath. 'I hadn't realised protests could become so—tense,' she confessed in sombre tones.

'Or that not all your group's allegations are necessarily the truth?' he asked subtly.

Revel's head lifted. 'If that's a reference to what was said earlier, then that's something else entirely,' she declared.

'Although if you're so sure we are felling unmarked trees, and *if* you believe as strongly as you claim that logging should be halted here, then I would have thought my offer to shut down the mill would have been sufficient encouragement to have you rushing to accept my invitation in order to prove your point.'

'By checking every log on the site?' Revel pulled an expressive face. 'And how many hours would that take?'

Tyler hunched a deprecating shoulder. 'Provided it enables you to discover the truth—does it matter?'

Revel heaved a vexed sigh, feeling as if she was being backed into a corner. 'But I've made other arrangements,' she all but wailed in protest.

'For which you require a set of wheels, I presume?' he drawled, mockingly implicit, and the reminder had her slumping in her seat defeatedly.

Of course, her car was bogged! And, what was more, she supposed she had little chance of even returning to it without his help. She couldn't even have said for certain exactly where it was!

'Meaning, I don't get my car back until I've been to the mill?' she assumed on a resigned note.

'Did I say that?' Tyler countered, but with such a suspicious degree of innocence that Revel didn't doubt that that was precisely what he'd had in mind.

'You didn't have to,' she muttered under her breath, turning her head away, although only until curiosity got the better of her and had her flicking him a quizzical glance. 'So why were you on that particular track anyway? To check on your equipment?' Whatever the reason, it had been fortunate for her, at least in saving her from a decidedly long and unpleasant hike in atrocious conditions.

'That, and to locate your own troublesome self, of course!' she was informed succinctly. 'You apparently told Hattie you would be home before dark.'

Revel bent her head. 'Yes—well—I'm sorry if she was worried, but thank you for——'

'Don't bother thanking me. I did it for Hattie,' Tyler broke in to impart squashingly. 'As far as I'm concerned, it would have been no more than you deserve if you'd had to remain out here all damn night!'

Revel's heart constricted painfully. All the same, he *had* shown consideration for her welfare, no matter what he claimed, she tried impressing on herself comfortingly, and for the short remainder of their journey gave her attention to the wet and shining ribbon of sealed road that they now followed.

CHAPTER SEVEN

As TYLER had predicted, the following morning was bright and clear once the early mist lifted. It was also considerably warmer than the day before, Revel was pleased to note.

A hot shower, dry clothes, and a nourishing meal the previous night had thankfully seemed to redress any ill effects she might have suffered from her icy drenching, but it still wasn't an experience she felt inclined to repeat. With this in mind, she decided that, since her prior arrangements for the day had already been nullified, after she had finished at the mill and was again in possession of her car would be as good a time as any to drive to town to purchase some rather more protective attire.

But now, after alighting from the ute she had shared with Tyler and his father for the journey to the mill, which was located on the outskirts of the town, and Ellis had bade them farewell and set off for the small hut that a sign above the door denoted as 'Office', Revel turned to his son with an ironic look.

'Well, where would you suggest I start?' she quizzed in dry tones. To her eyes the whole area appeared a confusion of stacks of both cut and uncut logs, as well as sawn timber.

Tyler flexed a broad, denim-jacketed shoulder. 'I wouldn't presume to advise you,' he drawled uncooperatively. A sardonic tilt caught at his mouth. 'You'd probably accuse me of attempting to direct you away from incriminating evidence.'

Revel pressed her lips together, and did her best to camouflage the dispirited feeling that swept over her. It

hadn't been long after their return to the house last night
that she had come to realise that Tyler and Ellis, too,
must have been made aware of, and acceded to Hattie's
dictate that she would have no dissension within the
house. As a result, she now realised that she had merely
allowed herself to be lulled into the false belief that
Tyler's earlier alienation might have begun to abate. His
last remarks made it apparent that it hadn't. That she
shouldn't have cared, she well knew, but then, for some
inexplicable reason, it seemed she'd had trouble controlling her feelings ever since she'd first met this man.

'All right, then I'll decide for myself,' she declared
summarily at last. 'It will doubtless take far longer, but
since it's your time we'll be wasting...' She forced a
chafing smile. 'Shall we go?'

Tyler shook his head sharply in veto. 'Except that I've
no intention of accompanying you. I've more important
work to be doing, and you don't need me around to be
able to tell whether a log's marked with a red circle or
not.'

Revel's lips parted, and she made an instinctive grab
for his arm when he made a move as if to depart. 'Oh,
no, you're not slipping out of it that easily, Tyler
Corrigan!' she flared indignantly. 'This was your idea,
and if it's good enough for my arrangements to be over-
ridden, then so can yours be as well! You said *you* could
prove it to me that no unmarked trees had been logged,
and that's precisely what you're going to do.'

'You being the one to force me into doing so, hmm?'
he mocked, gazing pointedly at the hand still gripping
his arm, and, with self-conscious colour suffusing her
cheeks, Revel withdrew her hand quickly.

'We both know the answer to that,' she granted flatly.
Just the idea of her being able to even match, let alone
overcome, his obvious physical strength was too ludi-
crous for words. 'And you're not being fair.'

'While all your actions to date have been, I suppose,' he had no compunction in retorting swiftly. 'And your seeming desire for a heinous logger's company this morning a handy ruse for keeping me occupied because you know what your friends will be up to elsewhere.'

'No!' Her widening turquoise eyes flew up to his again in resentful disbelief. 'And when it was you who insisted I come here that's a rotten accusation to make!' she railed, her voice strengthening. 'But if that's what you want to believe, then *don't* damn well accompany me! I think I'd rather see over the place on my own now, anyway.' Spinning on her heel, she began storming across the yard towards the furthest stack of uncut logs.

'Here! You should wear one of these.' A hard hat was abruptly placed on her head as Tyler caught up with her before she had even reached halfway. 'We wouldn't want you brained before you could vouch that we're not cutting unmarked trees.'

'Oh, I don't know. There would be at least some compensation for you... in having one demonstrator less,' she gibed promptly in return without either looking at him or slowing her step. Then, when he continued to keep pace with her, 'And I thought you had more important matters to attend to.' Now she did look at him scornfully. 'Or has it suddenly raised your suspicions that I might try my hand at a little sabotage if left to my own devices?' Her voice became imbued with caustic sarcasm.

'No, that hadn't occurred to me,' he denied with a shake of his head. He paused, exhaling heavily. 'And I apologise for what I said. I guess it wasn't merited.'

Mollified a little, Revel ventured to glance at him through her long, sweeping lashes. 'Then if suspicion wasn't the reason for you, apparently deciding to accompany me——' he was still walking alongside her, after all '—why did you change your mind?' she questioned tentatively, and Tyler's mouth suddenly sloped with a crooked tilt.

'I still haven't answered that to my own satisfaction yet,' he surprised her by advising on a self-mocking note, dragging a hand through his dark hair before clapping into place his own hard hat that he'd been carrying. 'I do have more urgent work that I should be doing.'

Revel averted her gaze, her pulse quickening at the implication in his words. Then, before her courage could desert her, owned in a throaty, deprecating voice, 'If it's of any interest, I missed your company yesterday.'

Beside her, she sensed rather than saw Tyler stiffen, and briefly the only sounds to be heard were those of the mill. 'That must have been very—discomfiting for you...and Renwick,' he returned expressionlessly at length, and she had to avert her gaze to hide the anguish that she knew must be visible in her eyes.

'Y-yes. Yes, it was,' she was nothing loath to agree in protection of her mortified emotions, although in such choking accents that her attempt to appear indifferent was completely destroyed. She had hoped his attitude might have been relenting, but evidently she couldn't have been more wrong! 'I thought you would find it amusing,' she added with a ragged half-laugh, and, watching her strained features, Tyler swore long and violently beneath his breath.

'Damn you to hell, Revel!' he went on just as savagely, bringing them to a halt by grasping her shoulders and swinging her behind one of the high stacks of sawn timber. 'Just what do you want—expect—of me? You chose Renwick and the opposition camp!'

Revel circled her lips with her tongue. He was so close that she could feel his breath warm against her skin, see the fine lines radiating out from the corners of his ebony-framed eyes—and the shapely mouth that she suddenly found her fingertips wanting so much to touch.

'Not Sebastian. Only the demonstration,' she found herself qualifying on a shaky breath—to her amazement. 'But that still doesn't mean we have to be mortal enemies...does it?' Lord, was that really her saying that? Just what had he done—was still doing—to her, this man whom she had fully anticipated disliking intensely?

Tyler drew back a space, his expression ironic. 'So what are you suggesting? Amicable enemies with an agreement to disagree?' He gave an incredulous shake of his head. 'For heaven's sake, it's my livelihood—and that of many others—you're trying to abolish! How the hell do you expect me to react? By making love to you?'

Revel's stomach tightened at the thought, her every sense attuned to the heat and power that emanated from his tautly held form, and before she was even conscious of the question forming the words were rolling softly from her tongue.

'Do you want to?'

Tyler stared at her for an unnerving second, his eyes glinting greenly with the turmoil the question caused, the muscles of his jaw clenching. 'Damn you—yes!' The hoarse admission seemed wrenched from him and, as if unable to help himself, he pulled her close with a hand at her nape, his mouth slanting across hers in a hard and searing kiss that vividly displayed an uncontrollable hunger which Revel was shaken to discover promptly kindled an answering craving within herself.

Their mouths suddenly became inseparable as desire, hot and overwhelming, flared between them, and, oblivious to their surroundings, Revel responded uninhibitedly. Beneath the fierce demand of his lips hers parted willingly, her tongue licking against his own as it ravaged the moist, sweet recesses made available to it.

Urgent, consuming, his mouth devoured hers until she was breathless and trembling with longing, her hands clinging to his shoulders for support as she felt the muscles in her legs beginning to wilt.

Then, just as abruptly as he had drawn her close, Tyler now set her away from him.

'I just wish to hell I didn't, that's all,' he groaned on a thickened, uneven note edged with self-disgust. 'An entanglement, of any kind, with a protester——' his jaw tightened '—particularly a devious one, is the last damn thing I either need, or want, right at the moment.'

Revel struggled for composure. 'You think my involvement with a *logger* is any easier to come to terms with?' she challenged in throatily eloquent tones. 'While as for what the other demonstrators' reaction might be, should they discover just where I happen to be staying...'

'You haven't told them?' He raised an explicit brow.

Revel looked away, executing the smallest of shrugs. 'I didn't consider it prudent. And, since my opposition to one suggestion has already had accusations of defending you levelled at me, I hate to think what further allegations any such information might engender if I were to disclose it now.'

'You don't think they may well see it as an advantage, having someone in the heart of the enemy camp?' Tyler countered, lightly mocking.

'To pass on pertinent information?' Just as he kept intimating! With her lips setting, her head angled higher. 'Except, as I've already told you, that was never my intention,' she denied resentfully. 'Even if you and your father and Hattie do still change the subject immediately you think I might learn something of interest,' the addition came with protective sarcasm. 'But, no matter whether you believe it or not, I would never abuse your father's and your hospitality in such a fashion. I do have principles, you know!'

'Although you could hardly expect us to deduce that when the actions of your mates up there——' a scornful gesture was directed towards the hills behind them '—have never been anything but *unprincipled*!' he was quick to retort in withering accents.

'Simply because they're against what you're doing to the forests?' Revel was equally swift to defend sardonically. 'And what do you mean by "never been anything but unprincipled", anyway?' she went on to demand with a frown. 'The demonstration only began last week——'

'This time.'

Revel blinked. 'This time?' she echoed distractedly, and, seeing her puzzlement, Tyler uttered a humourless half-laugh, shaking his head in disbelief.

'As I suggested last night—go back to the city, sweetheart,' he recommended in a wry drawl. 'You're out of your depth here with this lot, that's for sure.'

'And once again that's not for you to decide, Tyler,' she flared on an acrimonious note, much as she had the night before. 'Nor am I any more enamoured of being patronised.'

Tyler inclined his head and shrugged, more derisive than penitent as he proceeded to relay in aggravating accents, 'Your little group of extremists have been in the area before. They're continually mounting demonstrations, in the south-east of the State in particular. Only last time they were screaming for the virgin rain forest in the valley below here to be preserved.'

Revel remembered the area, and how beautiful it was, from when she had passed through it on her way to Mount Winsome. 'And so it should be,' she immediately asserted with feeling. 'It is precisely such untouched forests that conservationists are most concerned about.'

'Save that it doesn't happen to *be* virgin forest at all. It's been logged at least twice last century, and once this, *and* we have the records to substantiate it. Moreover, it doesn't even happen to be rain forest, in any case,' he countered drily.

Revel's lips parted. 'But of course it is! What else could it be with all those palms and ferns and such?'

'Wet sclerophyll forest is the correct scientific classification,' she was advised decisively. 'It may have some rain forest species as an understorey, but it's the genus of the trees which form the upper stratum that determine a true rain forest.' He paused, his eyes shading ironically. 'And, feeling so strongly about the subject, you did note of course that the majority of those were eucalypts—black butt, flooded gum, tallow-wood, blue gum.' There was another pause. 'And none of which grow in rain forests.'

Revel shifted restively, only too aware that her own scientific knowledge of this particular subject was zero, and unused to being so uncertain of her facts. In her own field she could hold her own with anyone.

'All right, all right!' she heaved. 'So my awareness of the different species leaves something to be desired, and it isn't rain forest in the valley below but wet scler... wet——'

'Sclerophyll,' he inserted helpfully, his mouth quirking, and had her temper flaring anew.

'That still doesn't mean it's not worth protecting!'

'Except that it *is* already protected,' his return was forcefully delivered. 'Both by the Forestry Service and the detailed logging plans we have to submit before we're allowed to even touch a single tree—anywhere!' A sardonic smile curved his lips. 'And that protection is working very well, evidently, since neither you nor your self-appointed experts of friends could apparently even tell that the area in question had been logged previously. While as for labelling it rain forest, well, that could simply be through ignorance, or——' his expression soured '—in the case of your lot, just a blatant attempt to manipulate people's emotions due to 'rain forest' having become one of the great catchwords of the last decade.'

Revel pressed her lips together. 'While you're just saying that in order to cast doubts on their validity!' she charged exasperatedly.

'Not without cause, wouldn't you say?' Tyler drawled in mocking tones. 'Or have some of the mainstream conservation groups actually put in an appearance at your camp?'

Revel dropped her gaze discomfitedly. 'Well—no—not yet, as far as I'm aware,' she was grudgingly forced to admit. Then, as an infuriatingly knowing smile began catching at the edges of his mouth, added hurriedly, 'Although Sebastian says they'll be joining us very shortly.'

'Mmm, that's also what he said when he was leading the protest in the valley.' He paused. 'But they didn't arrive then either.'

Revel expelled a temporarily defeated breath and, taking his agreement for granted, resumed walking towards the logs which she was there to inspect.

'So what happened in the end?' she enquired curiously. 'Did they manage to—er—halt the logging, anyway?'

Tyler shook his head. 'No, thank heavens.' His lips twisted expressively. 'Although not before giving us a load of hassles, as well as putting us to a lot of trouble and expense in order to prove our case. Which is probably why they're back again now.' A heavily caustic note entered his voice. 'Maybe they figure they'll have better luck against us with their current theme of saving the State forests from supposed destruction.'

'Only there's nothing "supposed" about it as far as Sebastian's concerned,' Revel's rejoinder came swiftly. Her lips pursed. 'And, looking at the number of logs here, how could anyone not agree with him? I mean, it has to be only a matter of time before the forest disappears completely when so many trees are being felled.'

'Implying—once again—that your knowledge on the subject is so much greater, while those of us who actually earn our living from the industry are too short-sighted, too greedy, or just too plain stupid to know what we're doing, I presume?' His lips levelled, his eyes snapping with impatience. 'Well, thanks for the vote of confidence in my intelligence, but I'm sorry to have to disappoint you, because no matter how many logs there are here at the moment—due to the fact that we've just begun logging blocks twenty-three and twenty-nine—we still only take out less timber than the forest can re-grow each year. It's called selective logging for sustainable yield! A long-standing practice, I might add, that is the reason the forests are still here now for people like you to demonstrate over.' He slapped a hand down on to one of the logs they had come to a halt beside. 'For crying out loud, they've been cutting their forests in Europe for centuries, and still people admire them, so why should it be any different here?'

Revel shrugged a shoulder deprecatingly. 'I guess that depends on whether those practices are really sufficient, and——' she hesitated '—whether they're actually adhered to.'

Her implication was obvious, and Tyler's response immediate. 'So have you found a log that's unmarked yet?' he demanded in coolly satirical accents, his powerful frame stiffening. 'Or would that be too much like expecting you to deal in facts for a change instead of baseless insinuation?'

Nettled, Revel refused to give ground. 'It hasn't been proven to be baseless yet,' she retorted. Then, 'And what do those arrows on the logs signify, in any case?'

'They indicate the direction in which the tree is to be felled in order to cause the least damage to the surrounding growth,' Tyler supplied summarily.

'And the numbers impressed in the ends?'

'All trees are numbered when they're felled. That's how Forestry checks we're only cutting those marked,' he inserted pithily. 'The other two figures denote the length and centre girth. Calculating them together gives the volume of the log and thus sets its value. We do have to pay a royalty for the timber we cut, you know. We don't get it for free.' Acid sarcasm surfaced in his voice, setting Revel's teeth on edge.

'I never would have guessed,' she gibed facetiously with a fulminating turquoise glare, and stalked around to the other side of the stack.

Thankfully, however, the remainder of her inspection was accomplished without any further such flare-ups. In fact, after a while she even felt composed enough to sound Tyler out—albeit with a somewhat stiff tentativeness, initially—regarding a couple of other concerns, and received equally controlled answers in reply, much to her relief.

'But surely, even if the forest can withstand it, don't you consider people are entitled to areas where trees can grow to giants and where nature, not man, decides what lives and what dies, and when?' she queried at the last.

'Sure,' he had taken her aback a little by readily acceding, if laconically and with a negligent shrug. 'And I think you'll find there's around forty million acres already set aside in this country, with more being added all the time, for just that purpose.' A brief pause, and then drily, 'They're called National Parks.'

Revel swallowed ruefully. She'd forgotten all about those.

Of course, part of the trouble, she mused, was that when she was with Sebastian his claims seemed more than reasonable. Yet, simultaneously, when she was with Tyler his arguments seemed eminently sound also.

The other part of the trouble, she was fast having to concede, to her disconcertion, was that she simply didn't *want* to be in confrontation with Tyler. A not particularly satisfactory situation, she had to confess, but one which she didn't appear able to do much about. Her feelings just seemed to have developed a will of their own, against which her mind's protest was proving unsettlingly futile.

'Well?' the subject of her recent reverie now quizzed as, finally, she checked the last of the logs in the yard. 'Did you manage to find any that were unmarked?'

Revel exhaled a deep breath. 'You know I didn't,' she granted defeatedly at length. 'I guess they must have made a mistake.'

Tyler uttered a cynical snort. 'Or were simply working on the basis that if you throw enough mud some will be bound to stick.' His lips twisted. 'It does wonders for their coverage in the media, and arouses the feelings of the populace in general no end.'

Revel shook her head. 'While all your statements are absolutely unimpeachable, I suppose,' she couldn't forbear retaliating with an expressive grimace.

'At least I can produce concrete scientific evidence in support of my assertions regarding forest ecology and the effects of current practices thereon. Not like your mob, who merely offer in corroboration the *claim* that they're right,' came the prompt retort in grimly derisive accents. 'And if you doubt that as well, then allow me to provide you with the proof.' Catching hold of her arm, he began propelling her towards the office. 'I'll give you copies of those same official scientific studies— which, I might add, your friends like to allege have never been carried out—and maybe then you'll be convinced. At the least they should provide you with some actual facts to compare against the doubtlessly impending allegations such as that last-ditch cry, "But it's the last unique stand of..." whatever. That's always guaranteed to generate public misgivings.'

Revel couldn't control the involuntary twitching of her lips. She had to admit that even to her mind that par-

ticular phrase had been slightly done to death. Though
as they entered the small, temporarily empty office, its
walls lined with grid-marked forestry maps, and Tyler
started extracting numbers of bound documents from
one of the two filing cabinets, nor could she resist a sardonic dig of her own.

'In other words, we should forget the whole thing because the timber industry's practices have never been
anything but meticulously correct?'

Tyler spared her a speaking glance before pulling open
another drawer. 'I didn't say that,' he denied, the barest
hint of wryness in his tone having Revel venturing to
face him in feigned, wide-eyed astonishment as she rested
her arm on the top of the cabinet and cupped her chin
in her hand.

'You mean, there have actually been occasions when
you could have been faulted?' she marvelled facetiously.

Once again Tyler's sable-lashed gaze locked momentarily with hers, and then he hunched a muscular
shoulder and continued adding more documents to the
pile already held against one forearm.

'Sure, loggers are fallible, the same as everyone else,'
he owned indolently. 'Which is precisely why protective
legislation was passed in the very early years of this
century and foresters appointed in order to prevent any
uncontrolled exploitation.' He hesitated and then
shrugged again. 'Although that's not to say there aren't
improvements still being made, and could be made even
today.'

Surprise had Revel's lips parting. 'Despite everything
you've had to say, you're admitting the forest is in danger
and that we have cause to protest, after all?' she gasped
incredulously.

Tyler's mouth shaped crookedly, although there was
nothing oblique in his reply. It was direct and decisive.
'Not on the grounds you're doing so,' he rebutted de-
flatingly. An impatient shake of his head. 'And why on

earth do you people always have to exaggerate so? I said there was room for improvement, not that the forest was in danger. There's a hell of a difference between the two! Hopefully these might enable you to recognise the distinction.' He thrust towards her the collection of documents that Revel found she required both arms to hold, and which briefly she regarded with a distinct lack of enthusiasm.

Just when was she supposed to find the time to read all of those, and, if they were couched in scientific terms, even understand them, if it came to that? But for the moment there were answers to other questions which she was far more interested, and eager, to hear.

'OK, perhaps I did overstate the matter somewhat,' she was willing to allow. 'So just what are these improvements that could be made, then ... and in which areas?'

In response Tyler tapped her under the chin with a tanned forefinger in a gesture that she suspected was meant to provoke. That it did, but a pulse-quickening awareness of his compelling attraction and overwhelming proximity as he leant towards her, rather than irritation, she found impossible to dispel.

'When you show an inclination—something your companions have never once displayed, or even suggested—to sit down and discuss the matter rationally, instead of emotionally, I'll let you know,' he drawled on a mocking note. 'And you'll be disappointed if you're hoping those improvements are of a major nature, because they're not.'

Revel circled her lips with the tip of her tongue. 'According to you,' she just managed to push out faintly.

'Mmm, but I'm not in the habit of lying...remember?'

'Implying I am?' Her voice strengthened.

Tyler's mouth turned up a little at one corner. 'Let's just say, your record isn't exactly the best in that regard.'

Circles of heat stained Revel's cheeks. Then just as quickly they disappeared again as she remembered something he'd said earlier. 'Although still not bad enough for you to distrust me entirely, all the same, apparently. You told me which blocks you were logging,' she reminded him triumphantly.

'Then I'll know where the information came from if your mates suddenly turn up there, won't I?' he countered in tones that seemed all the more ominous due to their very softness, and accompanied by another mockingly emphatic tap beneath her chin.

Revel could only stare at him in appalled dismay, and was abruptly unable to prevent herself from wondering if the information disclosed hadn't been solely for that purpose, after all.

Not that it really made any difference, and especially when the demonstrators' own searches could quite conceivably discover those particular areas where logging was actually taking place, anyway, without even an iota of help from her, she realised with an uncomfortable swallow.

Nor did the events of her afternoon do much to relieve Revel's feelings either, on discovering that it was the Ainsworths who owned the general store in Mount Winsome. Briony proved to be at best unhelpful, at worst downright obstructive when eventually Revel was once more in possession of her now rescued car and had made her way in to town for her intended purchases, necessarily from the general store since it appeared the most likely outlet for such apparel. She had noticed a couple of smaller clothing shops, but as the windows of these had displayed decidedly more fashion-conscious attire she had decided to bypass them.

Nevertheless, on entering the surprisingly large, and decidedly old-fashioned building with its heavy wooden counters and shelves, as well as time-worn and noticeably uneven plank flooring, she was disappointed to find Briony the only person in attendance. She had hoped, on noting the sign outside, that it might be another member of her family, or staff, at least.

'So what do you want?' was the older girl's opening on a less than civil note immediately she caught sight of Revel. 'Come to complain about me telling Tyler just how friendly you and Renwick are, have you?' A self-satisfied smirk made an appearance.

Revel gritted her teeth, trying her best not to give in to the temptation to indulge in a little sniping of her own, but thankful that there were no other customers present all the same. 'No, as it happens, I've come to buy some clothes,' she responded with a simulated air of indifference which promptly had Briony's green eyes narrowing.

'Realised you're wasting your time chasing Tyler now, have you?' she mocked, refusing to be side-tracked.

'Unlike you, you mean?' The taunting riposte, together with a chafing smile, sprang spontaneously from Revel's lips this time before she could even think of holding it back.

'H-how dare you?' Briony spluttered furiously, her face becoming suffused with hectic splashes of colour. 'I'm as good as engaged to Kirk Sutcliffe.'

Albeit only as second choice, Revel had no doubt. Aloud, there was a touch of facetiousness in her acknowledging, 'Oh, that's right. How could I have forgotten?' A limpid smile formed. 'Perhaps because your interest seems continually focused in Tyler's direction.'

'Because we happen to be a close-knit community that cares about one another!'

'Although about *some* a great deal more than others, apparently.'

'I see nothing to be ashamed of when it's necessary in order to save them from unwanted interlopers despicably attempting to worm their way into people's confidence under false pretences!' Briony blustered. Then, adopting a haughty stance as she struggled to regain her composure, and evidently wanting to change the subject herself now, 'Anyway, I can't imagine our clothing range being of any interest to someone like you. We supply workers, not city types.' She waved a dismissive hand in the direction of the street. 'Try the two fashion shops. They'd be more in your line.'

Revel only wished she could. 'Except that it is more serviceable clothing that I'm after,' she advised ironically. 'For a start, a parka, or a jacket that's waterproof rather than just water-resistant for preference. Would you have something like that?' Unfortunately it was difficult to tell for most of the stock was stored in an old-fashioned manner as well—folded and stacked on the shelves behind the counters. Apart from a few articles adorning the wall, the only clothes actually available for inspection were a rack of jeans—and men's jeans at that—and another smaller one of women's winter dressing-gowns.

'A women's waterproof jacket? In your size?' Briony gave a rejecting grimace. 'Oh, I shouldn't think so. In fact, I'm sure we haven't. We don't usually get much call for those.'

'Perhaps in a small men's size, then?' Revel suggested patiently.

Briony shook her head. 'No, we haven't had our full order of those delivered yet, and what we did receive have gone already.'

Revel sighed, beginning to wonder if the other girl would admit to having *anything* she might wish to purchase. 'Then I suppose it will have to be a parka, after all,' she put forward with markedly less forbearance. 'That *is* what's in those plastic bags on that shelf there, isn't it?' was the swift addition to pre-empt the blonde denying having any of those either.

'Well—yes,' Briony conceded with a distinct lack of enthusiasm. Ambling to the shelves in question, she stood surveying them and tapping a finger against her teeth. 'Although whether there's any in your size...'

Revel pressed her lips together. 'Perhaps if you checked...'

With a loud exhalation, the other girl proceeded to do so—at a snail's pace. 'No, there doesn't appear to be,' she relayed languidly at length.

'Well, a larger one, then!' Revel's temper was starting to fray. 'I want a thick sweater to wear under it, in any case.'

'Although only in a men's, and in a dark, work-manlike colour, I trust,' Briony proposed promptly with a smug little smile. 'That's all we have in the way of heavy sweaters at the moment.'

'I didn't for one minute expect otherwise,' quipped Revel with a sardonic smile of her own.

Her quest for more substantial footwear than her trainers, however, was even less successful, this time the excuse given being that only the very largest of the men's sizes were left in stock.

But at least she would be a little better prepared when next the weather changed, Revel consoled herself later when putting her purchases away. Even if her parka was a particularly unattractive shade of muddy yellow and reached almost to her knees, and the two sweaters she had decided upon in the end were not only rough and prickly, but were as dull as ditch-water as well.

CHAPTER EIGHT

'SO WHAT happened to you yesterday?' quizzed Sebastian dubiously of Revel the following morning on her arrival at the camp. 'I thought you were going to help us locate where they're logging. We were a vehicle short when you didn't turn up——' He broke off to call last-minute instructions to the driver of a crowded Land Rover as it was about to depart. Facing her again, he continued on a somewhat short note, 'We need all the numbers we can get, you know. We'd never be successful if we all just ignored the arrangements made and only turned up when it suited us.'

'Yes, well, I'm sorry, but it was unavoidable. I had some—er—trouble with my car,' she explained minimally if a little stiffly as a result of his tone. All right, so perhaps she could have put in an appearance in the afternoon instead of going to Mount Winsome, but she wasn't owned by his group, for goodness' sake! 'Although I do have some good news for you,' she went on in more normal accents after only a moment's hesitation and thinking to cheer him. 'They're not cutting unmarked trees, as you thought the other day.'

'And how would you know that?'

'Who says they're not?'

The first rapid question came from Sebastian, the second from another of the protesters milling around them, and Revel was pleased to be able to declare, 'I say they're not. Because I didn't entirely waste my time yesterday,' she asserted with a meaningful glance in Sebastian's direction. 'In fact, I went to the mill and personally inspected every log there. And I can assure you there wasn't one unmarked one among them.'

'That proves nothing!'

'They probably haven't brought them in yet, that's all!'

'Or they've already disposed of the evidence!'

'So why would they let you in there to inspect them, anyway?'

The vehemence, and the dismissive nature of the comments, as even more of those near by joined in, took Revel aback somewhat. She had anticipated relief and pleasure at her announcement, not out-of-hand disregard and disdain. She began to regret even having mentioned the matter, especially as now they all appeared to be waiting—suspicion predominant—for an answer to that last discomfiting question. Taking a deep breath, she began carefully.

'I happened to—um—meet the mill owners through the woman with whom I'm staying, and when I mentioned—well, accused really—them of cutting unmarked trees, they insisted I should check the logs at the mill in order to disprove the charge.' Which was, more or less, the truth of it. 'And there *weren't* any unmarked logs there,' she reiterated challengingly, looking to Sebastian.

'Although, since it was at their insistence, unfortunately it's more than likely to have simply been a clever attempt to con you,' he proposed regretfully. 'As someone said, they probably just haven't brought any of them in yet.'

It was Revel who rejected his claim this time, with a sharp shake of her head. 'How could it have been an attempt to con me?' she demanded with some asperity. 'I didn't make the accusation until the evening, when the mill had already been shut down for the night, and I was there when it first started up again the next morning. There was no time for any cover-up to have been arranged.'

'Then it must be that those particular logs are still lying out in the forest somewhere,' he returned smoothly.

'Must it?' Revel countered promptly, doggedly, her thought processes suddenly puzzling over another aspect of the matter. 'Then perhaps you could enlighten me as to one rather pertinent point. Which is, since you haven't as yet discovered *where* they're cutting, how on earth would you know *what* they're cutting?'

Again there were a number of responses, but it was Sebastian's she was interested in, and it was upon him that her glance remained as his features assumed a placatory expression.

'You're new at this. You don't know them the way we do,' he asserted reassuringly. 'But we have our ways and means of knowing. Besides, why wouldn't they indulge in such practices if they're allowed to get away with it?'

'Because it wouldn't be in their best interests?' offered Revel a touch sardonically. 'And why would they be allowed to get away with it anyway? From what I understand, the Forestry Service makes them account for every tree felled.'

Sebastian gave a dismissive grunt. 'If you can believe that!' He laid an arm across her shoulders in his customary fashion. 'No, take my word for it, we know what we're talking about. We're the only ones who really have the interests of the forests at heart. After all, that's precisely why we're all here—including you—isn't it?' he prompted, giving her an encouraging shake. 'To preserve them?'

'I guess so,' Revel conceded on a resigned sigh, despite being aware that, his rhetoric notwithstanding, Sebastian still hadn't provided any definite proof in support of his claim, but deducing that any attempt to pursue the matter further would only elicit more of the same. However, the episode did serve to forcibly remind

her of something Tyler had said the previous day, to the
effect that it was no argument to put forward in corroboration merely the claim that they were right.

'And now that's settled . . .' Sebastian went on cheer-
fully meanwhile, his attention evidently moving on to
other matters '. . . you didn't happen to see anything while
you were at the mill that might indicate which blocks
they're cutting at present, did you?' His gaze became
one of intent anticipation.

Revel swallowed convulsively, never knowing how she
managed to prevent her colour from rising betrayingly.
'Er—no, I—I'm sorry, I didn't,' she stammered awkwardly with false regret. When all was said and done,
she might have been told, but she hadn't actually *seen*
anything, she told herself bracingly. Besides, as she had
informed Tyler, she couldn't in all conscience betray any
confidences revealed by the Corrigans, irrespective of
how she might personally feel about the matter. And,
as previously, if she hadn't happened to be staying with
them, the demonstrators would have had to come by their
information in some other fashion, in any event.

None the less, Sebastian's disappointment at her reply
was evident, and then his expression darkened even
further as the man, Marvin, probed, 'Well, did you
happen to notice their security arrangements while you
were there, then?'

Still unsettled to some degree by the previous question,
momentarily Revel could only favour him with a rather
blank look. 'No, of course not. Why would I?'

'A very good question,' inserted Sebastian with a glare
in the other man's direction, which was met with a shrug.

'I only meant so we could check the logs for our-
selves—without them around,' Marvin relayed off-
handedly. 'Now that they doubtlessly believe the heat's
off them, I just thought an—er—unscheduled visit, as
you might say, could provide an entirely different result.'

'Well, no matter what the reason, while I was there my only interest was the logs I was inspecting, certainly not any security arrangements,' Revel advised crisply, unsure whether to believe his explanation or not.

'As anyone with any sense would have realised,' soothed Sebastian with another speaking glance at his companion. 'We've enough ideas in hand to keep us busy at the moment, anyway.' And he proceeded to detail—for the benefit of not only Revel but also those other protesters who weren't part of the camp—the plans that had been devised for that day.

In the main these consisted of setting up barricades, comprised of whatever dead timber they could find, on as many of the roads and tracks as they suspected the loggers might use.

It was hot and tiring work, particularly as the weather was fine and warm again, but it provided plenty of time for thinking and as the day progressed—disappointingly, once again without sight or sound of the loggers—Revel's thoughts became more and more occupied with Marvin's suggestion of an unscheduled visit to the mill, and, despite the apparent innocuousness of his stated reason for such stealth, she was filled with doubts.

Unfortunately, and notwithstanding Sebastian's claims to the contrary, she was increasingly coming to suspect that the other man wouldn't hesitate to use vandalism as a means for gaining their ends...and just how tempting a target might the mill be to someone willing to utilise such methods?

As a result, knowing that she couldn't simply adopt a wait-and-see attitude, and in spite of the feelings of disloyalty assailing her, she gave in finally to the urging of her conscience during dinner at the house that evening.

'Do you have any security arrangements for the mill?' she blurted abruptly after taking a bolstering mouthful of wine.

For an instant there was complete silence as Hattie and Ellis Corrigan stared at her in brow-raised surprise. By contrast Tyler's eyes immediately narrowed with suspicion.

'What's it to you?' he was also the one to counter swiftly, bluntly, in probing tones.

Revel swallowed and raised a deprecating shoulder. 'To me, personally, nothing,' she allowed carefully, feeling she had already said enough to warn them.

'*And*...?' Evidently Ellis didn't agree as he now intervened to prompt on a dark note. As Hattie had once said, the mill was very much *his* concern. Then, in a roughening voice, when she didn't immediately respond, 'For the love of heaven, girl, you can't just leave it at that! Just what acts of sabotage——?'

'Terrorism!' amended Tyler scathingly.

'—are they planning now?' his father continued without pause. 'You do realise that ours wouldn't be the first sawmill to be burnt to the ground when, *coincidentally*——' sarcastically accentuated '—greenies just happen to be demonstrating in an area?'

Revel shrank from the thought. Was it really something like that that had been in Marvin's mind? Plainly, she was going to have to elucidate a little further, after all.

'I—well—the group, as a whole, wasn't really involved,' she faltered. 'It was just one particular person——'

'Renwick?' speculated Tyler on a harsh note.

'No!' Revel denied hotly, and not without some taunting satisfaction. 'In fact, Sebastian was extremely annoyed when the matter was raised.'

'For having had the cat let out of the bag, I've no doubt,' Tyler mocked immediately.

About to make a retort of her own, Revel was beaten to it by Ellis suddenly interposing impatiently, 'Yes, well, if we could just get to the nitty-gritty...'

With a last glare across the table, Revel turned her gaze to the older man. 'One of the men made mention of an—um—unscheduled visit to the mill... when you weren't around. To check for unmarked logs, he claimed,' she added hurriedly, excusingly.

A disclosure which brought a scornful bark of disbelief from Ellis and from Tyler the furiously grated demand, 'You didn't tell them you'd already inspected them... and found every one legitimately marked?'

At the implied censure Revel's head lifted. 'Naturally I did!' she flared, and then, on recalling the ensuing reaction to her revelation, averted her gaze, biting at her lip. 'Unfortunately it only seemed to engender either uninterest and—or—rejection.'

A satirical twist caught at Tyler's lips. 'Proof often has that effect on them. Usually, in fact, where your little bunch of eco-terrorists are concerned!'

'They're not terrorists!' she repudiated, incensed. That was twice now that he'd made such comments. 'For your information, many of them are simply genuinely concerned, ordinary people of varying ages, who have never participated in a demonstration before in their lives.'

'But all of whom are misguidedly being led by a group of militant independents who have never been called upon to produce one bloody shred of scientific evidence to validate their spurious claims!' he fired back derisively.

His mockery made her boil. 'Spurious? Only yesterday you admitted that not everything was as it could, or should be!' Revel gritted, flashing him a fulminating glance.

Tyler dipped his head—goadingly—in acknowledgement. 'Of course! Nothing ever is perfect,' he quipped, his voice filled with such eloquent irony that her cheeks burned as much as her temper. 'But, as I also said yesterday, they're quite apart from your mates' claims. While as for their not being terrorists...' he leant his elbows on the table, his chin resting on his clasped hands

'...still sufficiently alarming, apparently, to have you seeing fit to issue a warning, none the less.'

Revel shifted discomfitedly. How could she gainsay that? In defence she could only insist with an astringent edge, 'Only about one of them!'

'Or the only one honest enough to advise their intentions,' came the prompt rejoinder.

'And, be that as it may,' Hattie now joined in for the first time, with some asperity, '*I* said I'll have no dissension in the house over these matters!' A fiercely emphasising glance swept around the table, and received three varying reactions in response.

Revel chewed at her lip contritely while a hint of conspiratorial amusement unexpectedly filled Tyler's eyes as they locked with the turquoise blue pair across the table that had so recently been sparkling irately at him, and Ellis leant forward urgently in his chair, regarding the older woman with a frown.

'But there's more than just a demonstration at stake here now, Hat!' he protested.

'Then go and do something about it!' she recommended—or was it ordered?—sardonically, and was repaid with a droll look.

'I was intending to,' he advised in dry accents. 'It's just that young Revel may know——'

'Now!' Hattie interjected succinctly.

Ellis lifted his eyes ceilingwards, as if seeking help. 'Damned bossy woman!' he muttered ruefully to no one in particular. Then, with a shake of his head, he lowered his glance to his son. 'I don't know how we put up with her all these years.'

'Because you couldn't do without me,' Hattie had no hesitation in speaking up on her own behalf wryly.

'You're supposed to wait for others to say that,' he chided on a bantering note, pushing back his chair.

'I haven't got that many years left if I've to wait for you to do so!'

'You wound me! After the way I've always——'

'Go! Just go!' Hattie pointed dramatically to the doorway, and he rose to his feet with a long-suffering sigh.

'Impossible woman!' It was obvious that he didn't mean to go silently. And, directing his gaze to his son once more, lamented, 'They're all the same.'

'You can say that again,' Tyler had no compunction in agreeing, casting an unwavering glance straight across the table, which had the smile that had been hovering about Revel's mouth during the others' exchange swiftly fading.

'And you can take him with you!' It was another dictate from Hattie with a nod to indicate the younger man. She suddenly gave a speaking smile. 'I've no doubt Revel, at least, will enjoy the respite.'

A remark which promptly had Revel's own smile returning in full force as Tyler also gained his feet.

'I was going, in any event,' he drawled mockingly, although instead of immediately joining his father and making for the doorway he halted at the head of the table, his expression sobering as his gaze sought Revel's. 'Notwithstanding anything said, we do thank you for your warning, all the same.'

'That's the truth, lass,' endorsed Ellis quickly, sincerely, and, with her own features taking on a more serious cast once more, Revel made a deprecating gesture.

'I've never held with the idea that any means justifies the end,' she said quietly, fighting to subdue the idiotically warm feeling that Tyler's appreciation had started within her. For goodness' sake, she was here to oppose him, not to seek, or bask in, his approval!

Nevertheless, it proved a waywardly difficult feeling to dispel, even after he and his father had departed. In fact, to her disconcertment, it stubbornly remained to buoy her throughout the hours they were gone. As a result, when she finally heard the sound of their vehicle returning, just as she had retired to her room for the night, she hurriedly re-donned the shirt and jeans which she had only seconds before removed, and headed for the stairs.

She could hear Tyler's and Hattie's voices coming from the kitchen, that woman evidently a little slower than planned in seeking her own bed, but Revel had only just started down the steps when Tyler suddenly swung into view below to begin mounting them two at a time. And the implied urgency of his action had her stopping abruptly, anxiety making her reach out to grip the banister involuntarily.

At almost the same time Tyler caught sight of her and, although his steps slowed, they didn't stop. 'Hattie said you'd gone to bed,' he relayed as eventually he came to a halt on the step below her, though that still only succeeded in putting her eyes on the same level as his.

Revel waved her free hand vaguely. 'I heard the ute...' Suddenly aware that there was complete silence in the kitchen now, she put forward apprehensively, 'Your father—he didn't come back with you?'

Tyler shook his head. 'Uh-uh! He decided to stay.'

'Everything is all right, though?'

Tyler half smiled and took her by surprise when he traced the line of her jaw with a lingering forefinger. 'It will be...thanks to you,' he conceded on a slightly deeper note, and, whether in relief or because of the effect of his caressing touch, Revel sank down weakly into a sitting position. 'We've made arrangements with a security firm in Brisbane to handle the matter and they'll have some of their men up here in the morning,' he went on to advise, lowering his lithe length on to the stair beside her. 'Meanwhile the old man and a couple of the others will do the honours tonight, with the police putting in an extra appearance or two.'

Revel nodded. 'The way you started up the stairs, I thought... Well, you just looked so intense,' she recalled heavily.

'Everything about you seems to engender an intense reaction in me.' His return was wryly voiced. His mouth shaped crookedly at her puzzled look. 'It was you I was on my way to see.'

'Oh!'

'Mmm; since it was at your instigation, I thought it more than likely you could be interested in the outcome.'

'Thank you.' With the beginnings of a half-smile catching at her mouth, she indicated her position on the stairs meaningfully. 'As you can see... I was.'

Tyler nodded faintly, his gaze lingering on the upward curve of her lips in such a disturbingly intimate contemplation that she suddenly found it difficult to breathe. 'It's we who should be thanking you, particularly as I can imagine how hard a decision it must have been for you to warn us,' he declared softly, his words unrelated to the warm huskiness of his voice.

Revel swallowed, all too conscious now of the hard muscularity of his thigh as it brushed familiarly against hers. 'I would have done the same if the positions had been reversed, and—and you've already thanked me,' she pushed out unevenly.

'Then I guess there's nothing more to be said,' he reflected, but without showing the slightest inclination to leave. Instead he lifted a hand to toy with her hair meditatively.

Revel bent her head. 'I suppose not,' she acceded reluctantly, making no move either.

'Except to say...'

'Yes?' she prompted with mortifying eagerness and expectancy when he didn't immediately continue, her eyes flying swiftly upwards again.

Tyler captured her head between his hands, his fingers pushing into her hair. 'Just that I wish to hell you'd never become involved with that mob,' he growled in throaty tones, his breath sensuously warm against her skin, and Revel circled her lips with the tip of her tongue.

'Because you can't take the opposition?' she put forward raggedly, her pulse beginning to quicken.

Tyler's eyes darkened. 'From you—no,' he owned thickly, his mouth grazing the corner of her parted lips. 'I want you on my side, and by my side. Just like this.' His lips sought the sensitive underside of her jaw and the throbbing cord beneath her ear now, and Revel quivered, feeling her every sense come alive in response.

As always, she had no defences against him, and when reciprocal feelings stirred within her she could only moan on a helpless sigh, 'Ty...'

'It's been a while since you called me that,' he murmured, his mouth finding hers again, tantalisingly, arousingly, in a succession of kisses that had her instinctively moving closer.

'I wasn't sure you wanted me to any more,' she confessed huskily, sliding her arms around his neck.

Tyler traced the contours of her lips with his thumb. 'I wasn't sure I did either,' he relayed, his mouth quirking whimsically.

'And now?'

'You really need me to tell you?' He shook his head. 'I thought I'd always made it more than plain exactly what you do to me—no matter which damned side you're on!' As if in confirmation, his lips closed on hers in a fiery, probing kiss of desire that Revel responded to with an aching depth of feeling which she had never before experienced.

If he was attempting to subvert her, he was coming very close to succeeding, she realised dazedly, her mind whirling and her conscience regarding Sebastian and the demonstration receding like the ebbing tide.

Nor could she ignore the fact that she wanted him with an intensity that she hadn't believed possible;

wanted him to bury himself within her, and to relieve the spiralling need that was building until her thighs ached with it.

It seemed to overtake them so swiftly—searing, consuming passion—in an explosion of feeling that turned their breathing ragged. Kiss after ravishing kiss sent fluid fire coursing through Revel's veins and set her moving against him in an unconsciously open invitation.

Suddenly she found her shirt undone and Tyler's mouth and hands sensuously exploring her heated flesh even as her own hands slid beneath his sweater to seek the same arousing intimacy with him. His skin was smooth and tautly moulded over the rippling muscles it covered, and she luxuriated in the feel of latent power evident in every movement.

Yet, despite their obvious strength, his hands were amazingly gentle as they stirred and intoxicated in their wanderings until her body was throbbing with a longing that was only partially satisfied when his lips closed over each of her already swollen nipples in turn.

Teasing and sucking, his mouth tormented her with exquisite sensations that had her moaning her pleasure aloud and her fingers kneading the muscles of his back convulsively, uncaring of the time and place, of everything except him.

'Dear lord, what you do to me...!' Tyler groaned hoarsely, shaking his head in disbelief as he touched his fingers to her flushed cheek. His mouth tilted. 'And you thought it was possible to prevent a relationship developing between us?' A slight pause. 'Renwick, and his protest, or no.'

'We've still only known each other for just a week,' Revel breathed, but whether in attempted warning, or merely incredulity, she was in no state to decide.

'Although still long enough to know I want you... as I've never wanted anyone else in my life before,' he confessed in a deep voice heavy with emotion.

'As I want you, too,' Revel owned in a shaky whisper, tracing the contours of his shapely mouth with a fingertip, and he turned her hand in order to press his lips caressingly against her palm.

Then, abruptly, they were springing apart and Revel frantically righting her clothes as the sound of a footstep in the hall below, abnormally loud in the emotion-charged atmosphere, penetrated their consciousness and they discovered Hattie heading for the stairs.

'You're still up? I thought you must have gone to bed,' that woman remarked casually on starting up the steps, and Revel couldn't prevent the rush of self-conscious colour that washed into her cheeks as she and Tyler proceeded to follow Hattie upwards.

Irrespective of the innocence of the comment, those last words had too closely resembled her own wishes for comfort.

CHAPTER NINE

FOR the next week the demonstrators went about erecting ever more barricades, as well as manning those already erected.

Not being as conversant with the forest as the loggers, their efforts to locate the blocks being cut were proving frustratingly unfruitful. Or, that was, until just after midday the following Friday when, it seemed to Revel, all hell broke loose.

'We've found them! We've found them! They're on block twenty-nine!' the triumphant shout went up as a pair who had been doing some scouting raced back to the camp, and for a while pandemonium reigned as people scurried in all directions, heading for vehicles and setting off for the logging site. And close behind them followed the TV crews and the police.

As usual Revel found herself accompanying Sebastian, but this time somewhat apprehensively. Not only was she nervous about just what was likely to happen when the two opposing factions came face to face, but it was with extreme trepidation at the thought that, of all places, it just had to have been block twenty-nine, and that as a result Tyler might believe she had been the one to disclose their location.

Even armed as they were with a map similar to those Revel had seen in the mill office, it still took them some time to reach their destination. Then ahead of them they suddenly saw logs from a pile at one side of the track being loaded on to a waiting timber-hauler, and almost before their own vehicle had been brought to a halt diagonally across the track to block the truck's exit the doors had been thrown open and people were spilling out.

'Come on! Now's your chance to really do something to help achieve our aims,' Sebastian shouted to her above the increasingly raised voices as more, from both sides, arrived—including a forbiddingly tight-lipped Tyler, noted Revel with a hollow feeling, and shortly thereafter another police vehicle with reinforcements—and he began urging her towards the loader, where she was propelled into clambering on to one of the projecting tines along with him, as others were doing, to prevent the driver from scooping up another log from the pile.

With the TV crews now in action, and the police doing their best to impose some sort of control as tempers began to flare and haranguing matches started, the atmosphere was close to flash-point, and Revel found herself wondering just how she had come to be in the forefront of something so volatile. The more so when she remembered her contention to her mother that she wasn't planning anything so dramatic as throwing herself in front of any machinery!

'But this really isn't what I had in mind, Sebastian,' she protested in consequence, trying to leave her position, only his hand in the middle of her back kept her pinned there. 'I'm sorry, but I'd much rather make my dissent known a little less spectacularly.'

'Maybe, but it's the spectacular that grabs the public's attention,' he declared vehemently, his eyes darting hither and thither in order to keep track of what was happening elsewhere. 'Oh, good, they've got the cameras on us now.' The insertion was made with almost hand-rubbing satisfaction. 'With your face being so recognisable—one of the influential and politically involved Ballards, no less—it will add a lot of weight to our cause,' he all but crowed.

Shocked at the implication, Revel twisted her head to look at him over her shoulder—with difficulty since the machine was still edging towards the pile of logs. It was a similar remark to the one the TV interviewer had made that first day, and she liked it no more now than she had then.

'But my presence here has nothing to do with my family,' she remonstrated angrily. A sudden, resentfully acrimonious thought occurred. 'Or was the fact that I was a Ballard really the main reason you were so keen to have me join your demonstration in the first place?'

'Oh, of course not,' Sebastian denied, but without looking at her, and not altogether satisfactorily convincingly to Revel's mind. 'The more there are the better, but, whether you like it or not, naturally a member of a high-profile family will assist in——'

'Giving credibility to a protest that might otherwise generate little interest?' she interposed tartly. When all was said and done, still no members of any of the main conservation groups had put in an appearance as yet.

Now Sebastian did deign to return his gaze to her narrowly. 'So why should you care...*if* you're as interested in halting logging as you claim to be?' he snapped on a derogatory note.

Revel stiffened. 'Because I object to being used!' she retorted hotly, and, with a concerted effort, this time managed to pull free of his hold and scrambled clear of the loader.

And just in time, she observed in some relief on seeing the police now beginning to prise some of the others from their similar perches forcibly. No matter how flippant her comments might have been to her mother, being hauled off in a police van really wasn't something she contemplated lightly—not least of all out of respect for her family, and consideration of her own position within the family firm. That there were many present who had no such qualms was evident, however, in the numbers willing to immediately take the places of those being removed.

Around Revel the activity, the chanting, and the verbal tirades between the two sides continued unabated—some of the latter even appearing to be on the verge of degenerating to a physical level until the intervention of the harassed police. And it was as she moved to avoid one such developing confrontation that she abruptly found herself face to face with Tyler.

'You double-dealing bloody jade! You've done it to me again, haven't you?' he snarled without preamble, raking her with a contemptuous gaze, although it was difficult to determine whether his anger was mostly reserved for her—or himself. He nodded sharply to indicate the turmoil about them. 'Doubtless this is a return favour for the one you did us!'

'No! That's not true!' Revel denied hoarsely, despairing of the fact that there wasn't a trace of any previous softness in either his eyes or his expression. It had been so different during the last week when his attitude had almost reverted to how it had been at the start. 'You must know that right from the beginning they've had people out searching to locate where you were working,' she went on in an effort to convince him.

'Although unsuccessfully... until you decided to take a hand, huh?' His sarcastically grated return made it obvious that she had failed in her objective, and she shook her head in vehement rebuttal.

'It was nothing to do with me!' Her dark lashed turquoise eyes sought his entreatingly. 'Ty, you have to believe that.'

'Why?'

'Because it's the truth!'

Tyler gave a sharp bark of cynical laughter that stabbed her with throat-tightening pain. 'And what would you know about that, when your entire presence here has been based on *untruths*? With us... and them!' he disparaged derisively in raw tones. A dark brow arched satirically high. 'Or have you actually come clean finally in that latter regard and told them with precisely whom you happen to be staying?'

Revel shifted discomfitedly, her gaze turning anxious as she glanced about them swiftly in alarm at the thought that they might be overheard. Thankfully, however, everyone else appeared fully occupied with his or her own form of confrontation, and she was able to breathe a little easier on that score at least.

In contrast, in answer to his question, she could only stammer lamely, 'Well—no—it didn't seem—appropriate.'

A muscle rippled alongside Tyler's jaw. 'Not the way it was when you declaimed to us about not endorsing the idea that any means justifies the end, hmm?' His lips curled disdainfully.

Confused, Revel stared back at him with a frown knitting her forehead. 'I don't understand,' she replied, puzzled, moving her head from side to side.

Tyler smothered a savage expletive and jammed splayed hands on to his hips. 'Well, what do you think this staged, attention-seeking stunt is, then, but the use of any means to enforce your minority will on others?' he slated corrosively, and she shivered at the explosiveness of his anger. 'Others, I might point out, who have to accept what the government decrees concerning our forests, so why the hell shouldn't you lot have to abide by the same laws?' It was a furious denunciation, not a question. 'But no, the rights of others are nothing, as far as you're concerned, when there's the chance to make as much media capital as possible out of something like this!' A sweeping hand furiously indicated the happenings around them. 'And you along with the worst of them! For all your alleged convictions, I noticed you couldn't wait to do your part by jumping on the loader in order to prevent the driver from continuing with his *legitimate* work!'

Revel gasped. 'But not from choice,' she hastened frantically to assure him. 'I was propelled into it before I realised what was happening.'

'Yeah?' Both his tone and expression were patently, dispiritingly disbelieving. 'I don't recall seeing you making any attempt to object.'

Revel's head lifted. 'I'm not still there, am I?' she retorted meaningfully, but Tyler merely flexed a dismissive shoulder.

'No doubt only to avoid being physically removed by the police,' he gibed in a voice hard-edged with scorn. His mouth levelled. 'Or maybe it was just that the arm Renwick had around you disappointingly slipped?'

'Or I was at last able to extricate myself from his imprisoning hold,' she countered forcefully after briefly pausing to wonder if it had been resentment that had brought about that last sniping remark. A conjecture which she had promptly rejected as wishful thinking. He didn't need resentment of a personal nature to make his feelings known regarding this mêlée!

'So you claim,' Tyler returned snidely, the disdain in his voice cutting, and Revel's shoulders drooped as a wave of swelling despair washed over her.

'Because it's true!' she choked, the sudden sting of unanticipated tears making their presence felt beneath her eyelids. Averting her gaze, she gave a helpless shake of her head. 'But you're just determined not to believe anything I say.'

'I wonder why.' His voice sliced at her harshly, caustically, and in reprisal had her eyes snapping back to his tautly set features instinctively.

'Probably because you're averse to admitting you just might be wrong!' she flared on an anguished, accusing note.

Fleetingly Tyler regarded her in silence, his expression unreadable as he took in her misty, shimmering gaze.

Then his jaw clenched and he grated roughly, 'In which case you have only yourself to blame.'

Revel bit at her lip to halt its humiliating trembling. 'For ever having become involved with someone so distrustful and so—so inflexible...you couldn't be more right!' she threw back at him brokenly, and turned on her heel to prevent him from seeing that her tears had begun to spill uncontrollably on to her cheeks now—only to discover herself staring straight into the lens of a TV camera.

'So the destruction you've found here has affected you to such an extent that you've been moved to tears?' immediately came the unashamedly eager proposal from the interviewer accompanying the cameraman.

For a brief second Revel could only stand there, seemingly transfixed by the red light on the camera which revealed that it was recording, and wishing she had never heard of the Mount Winsome State Forest.

But it was obvious that something had to be said—she strongly doubted that the interviewer would be prepared to forgo an answer—although in the end it wasn't to him that she directed her reply. That was reserved for Tyler, with a compulsive and pain-filled look of reproach over her shoulder.

'Unjustified abuse, in any form, has always had a similar effect on me,' she asserted on something like a sob, and knew from the way Tyler's muscular frame tensed, and the sudden glitter in his narrowing eyes, that he at least was aware that her words were meant for him.

For herself, Revel only wanted to escape, particularly from further attention by the media, and, brushing past them hurriedly, she sought relative anonymity among those who were milling around the police vans, heckling the blue-clad officers as they incarcerated some of the more resistant of the protesters within the vehicles.

'Say, that was great! It'll look sensational on the news tonight!' exclaimed Sebastian in satisfaction as he abruptly appeared at her side. 'You couldn't have done better if it'd been scripted. Tears and "unjustified abuse".' He hooted delightedly. 'Wow! If that doesn't create outrage, and help bring these rapacious profit-mongers to their knees, nothing will.'

Revel wiped her still wet eyes with her fingers as if to clear her vision in order to see him better. 'Bring them to their knees?' She shook her head confusedly. 'I thought your sole interest was in the trees.'

'Well, of course it is,' he was quick to aver. An indifferent shrug followed. 'But if we're to put a halt to logging there's bound to be some casualties along the way, so why shouldn't it be these get-rich-quick merchants who've been ruthlessly devastating the environment for *their* gain all these years?' He shrugged again. 'And obviously you feel the same, or you wouldn't have been in tears and said what you did about the devastation you've seen here this afternoon.'

Revel rubbed a hand across her forehead as her glance spontaneously swept the area. Admittedly there were a few stumps of newly felled trees visible, and the two tracks had been somewhat churned up by the machinery, plus some of the scrubby vegetation flattened, but . . . devastation?

'But—but that wasn't exactly to what I was—um—referring,' she stammered uneasily, suddenly realising the possible ramifications of her protectively double-edged but unthinkingly voiced remark.

'Oh, well, no worries.' Sebastian apparently had no such concerns. 'Whether you meant here, or somewhere else, the effect will still be the same, and that's all that matters.' He paused, an intent look coming over his face as his gaze alighted on the TV crew now filming the filling vans. 'But what will really put the icing on the cake is a shot of you now being carted off by the police for your convictions,' he declared animatedly, and before she could do more than open her mouth to make an appalled protest she had been hustled to the forefront of those attempting to hinder the police in carrying out their duty.

And it was purely automatic—if imprudent in the circumstances—that when a heavy hand promptly fell on her shoulder Revel immediately started struggling to free herself.

'No! I was pushed into this,' she tried to explain on a panted note as she was hauled inexorably towards the van.

'Sure you were,' came the openly sceptical and long-suffering reply. 'Only I happen to have seen you on the loader earlier, and, as far as I'm concerned, you're one of the leaders, girlie.' Without further ado she was thrust ignominiously into the back of the barred van with Sebastian following closely after her.

'So what happens now?' Revel demanded of him in heaving tones as the doors clanged shut behind them and they settled themselves as comfortably as possible amid the others already inside. She really was incensed with him for his arbitrary action. 'I suppose we end up in court, being fined.'

'No, they've changed their tactics these days,' someone else advised. 'I think they figured that was giving us too much media coverage, as well as congesting the court system.' He grimaced. 'So now they usually just take us a couple of miles out of town and turn us loose.'

'That way it gets us out of the loggers' hair for some time, so they can resume working while we make it back to camp,' Sebastian now added rancorously. 'And tomorrow they'll change the area they're working, which puts us to the trouble of locating them again.'

Revel nodded, thankful, at least, for the small mercy that she apparently wasn't going to have to appear in court and, consequently, gradually beginning to feel a little better disposed towards the man next to her.

'But your own vehicles?' she quizzed, reminded of them as she looked out through the darkened window on feeling the van start to move off. 'What happens to them?'

'Oh, they mostly only round up those of us offering resistance,' Sebastian elucidated. 'A warning to move out of the area is usually sufficient to have the rest dispersing, so they'll take the vehicles back to camp.'

'I see,' she murmured absently, her attention returning to what was happening outside as the van began to pick up speed.

Or, more particularly, to see what Tyler was doing, she acknowledged dejectedly with a sigh. Although why she should be interested, especially after what had happened, she really didn't know.

She tried to assure herself that she didn't care, but a treacherous knot of tension in her stomach kept proving otherwise. And never more so than when he happened to glance at the departing van with eyes that snapped with a savage look and his mouth promptly settled into a hard and formidable line.

She had been wondering if he knew of her detention by the police, but, judging by his expression, she now guessed despondently that he was only too aware. She also surmised that it didn't augur well for a singularly pleasant encounter the next time they met.

As a result Revel found herself delaying her return to the house until it was well into the evening, and a number of hours after she, along with her fellow demonstrators, had finally made her way back to the camp.

Now, after parking her car, and crossing the intervening space with dragging footsteps, she sucked in a couple of deep, fortifying breaths before reluctantly entering the house by the usual way through the family room, and discovered her reception to be even worse than she had imagined as she took in the faces turned towards her. Tyler, looking no less tense than when she had seen him last; Ellis, seeming to be struggling to hold his tongue; and Hattie, wearing an expression that was a mixture of censure and reproach.

'Revel, how could you?' It was Hattie who broke the suspenseful silence first, and in such a disappointed tone that it immediately had the recipient of her disapproval casting Tyler a resentful glare.

'But I had nothing to do with——' she began.

'"*Unjustified abuse*"!' she was cut off by Ellis abruptly thundering as if unable to restrain himself any longer. '*What* unjustified bloody abuse?'

Revel swallowed and touched her teeth to her soft lower lip. So that mortifying episode evidently had made it into the news, just as Sebastian had hoped. Although exactly whose fault had that been, anyway? she reminded defensively. Her head lifted.

'That of your son!' she retorted defiantly, sending another speaking glance in the younger man's direction. 'If he hadn't been so pigheadedly determined to believe the worst——'

'That's supposed to be an excuse?' It was Tyler himself who interrupted her this time, in scornfully stinging accents.

Revel's breasts rose and fell sharply. 'No, not an excuse... the reason!' she retaliated fiercely.

'Mmm, the reason for you to do your bit for "*the cause*"!'

'That's a damn lie, and you know it!' A traitorous burning sensation began to make itself felt behind her eyes again. 'What was I supposed to say when——?'

'How about the truth?' he was quick to insert in witheringly sarcastic accents. 'That would have been a novelty for you, if nothing else.'

A sob caught in Revel's throat. 'I didn't think you'd appreciate having it advertised to all and sundry just what an unyielding bastard you can be!' she choked bitterly, and sensed rather than saw the startled movements of the two older occupants of the room.

Meanwhile Tyler rose to his feet so swiftly, and with such force, that his chair skidded backwards. 'Nor, no doubt, what a deceitful, conniving bitch you are, if I'd had my say! The media does, just occasionally, ask us for comments, too, you know,' he relayed with biting mockery as he paced wrathfully closer, and making her eyes widen doubtfully at his approach. 'But no, you preferred to add fuel to the fire with another baseless and typically exaggerated, emotion-exploiting allegation, uncaring of whose lives you could be helping to ruin in consequence.' He drew a harsh breath. 'It's not just those directly employed in the timber industry who lose their jobs when logging's halted, but hundreds of others in support and spin-off industries as well.'

'Then maybe you should have been more willing to believe me in the first place when I said I had no part in revealing where you were working,' Revel defended distraughtly, and not a little distractedly, his image blurring through the tears that waywardly misted her eyes, but which she resolutely refused to shed. He had succeeded in reducing her to tears once that day, and that had been disastrous enough!

'I don't believe this!' Ellis abruptly re-entered the conversation, leaping to his own feet and looking stunned. 'You're saying that's what's at the root of your touching performance on TV? Not logging, not the forest...but a petty bloody squabble with Ty?'

Revel shifted from one foot to the other. 'I—well— more or less, I suppose,' she owned falteringly. Then, with her voice firming, 'Only it wasn't petty to me.'

'Good lord almighty, girl, when compared to——' He broke off with a despairing shake of his head and, uttering an exasperated epithet as his eyes turned skywards, slumped back into his chair again.

'Oh, Revel!' it was left to Hattie to rebuke sadly. 'Don't you realise that, quite apart from anything else, and whether you actually believe the forests have been misused or not—let alone can produce proof—the credibility given to your comment would increase immeasurably should it now ever become known that you're staying with us? It would just automatically be assumed you were privy to information supporting your claim.'

'Whereas, in actual fact, you know so little about forests, you wouldn't know what claims to make, unless somebody else—with his own axe to grind—put the words into your mouth for you!' interjected Tyler derogatorily.

'That's not true! Although, even if it were, at least it wouldn't prevent me from recognising a length of tall timber that needs felling when I see it!' Revel was quick to retort, surveying him explicitly from head to toe, and then returned her attention to Hattie. 'I'm sorry,' she said in a small voice, including Ellis in her glance. 'It seems I'm the last one who should be throwing stones, in view of the way I've abused your hospitality.' She bent her head. 'I'll go and p-pack.'

Her voice started to break at the last and she rushed from the room and up the stairs to the privacy of her room, where the tears that had been threatening refused to be suppressed any longer. Forgetting about her packing, she simply threw herself on the bed and gave in to the anguish that was welling up inside her in unstoppable, dark waves.

Oh, hell, why did everything have to become so tangled? she despaired. It was obvious that she should never have agreed to stay in the first place. And if it hadn't been for Ty... She buried her head in her pillow as a fresh paroxysm of sobs racked her just at the mere thought of him.

Damn, *oh, damn*, when had he managed to assume such importance in her life that simply to clash with him could occasion such misery? She should have been hating him as a despoiler of the forests, for always being so ready to believe the worst of her... not feeling as if she was some sort of defector!

For how long her tears continued to fall, Revel had no idea, but it was the shock of a hand suddenly touching her shoulder that finally had her gasping to a halt and, looking up, found Hattie bending over her.

'I did knock, but I guess you—er—didn't hear me,' that woman said quietly, and with an imperceptible shake of her head Revel hurriedly brushed the dampness from her flushed cheeks as she sat up quickly and swung her legs over the side of the bed.

'I'm sorry,' she murmured throatily, her head bent. 'I should be getting on with my packing.' She made as if to rise, but a determined hand on her shoulder arrested the movement as Hattie seated herself on the bed beside her.

'That's precisely why I came to see you,' she relayed briskly. 'To stop you doing anything so impulsive.'

Now Revel did look up. 'But you said——'

'I know what I said,' Hattie cut her off with an impatiently waved hand. 'But, good heavens, that didn't mean I was implying you should leave.'

Revel hunched a diffident shoulder. 'What you said was right, though,' she contended in husky tones. 'And—and I think it would be more satisfactory all round if I did leave.' A shuddering sigh escaped. 'I guess I should never have agreed to stay in the first place, really.'

'Because of the conflict it's brought you into with Ty?'

Flustered, Revel averted her gaze once more, beginning to give an excess of attention to a thread protruding from the seam of her shirt-sleeve. 'Mr Corrigan would prefer to see the last of me, too, I'm sure,' she parried in a discomforted whisper.

'Implying that that's what Ty wants too?'

Revel made a deprecating movement. 'Well, doesn't he?'

'Has he ever said so?'

'He doesn't have to!' The words burst forth on a disconsolately quavering note. She struggled for some semblance of control. 'It—it's plain in his manner, and—and the way he refuses to believe anything I say.'

'Or you prefer to believe so because it's a convenient excuse for running away?'

Revel's throat constricted. 'I don't know what you mean,' she hedged, and Hattie's gaze turned askance.

'Oh, come on, Revel, you should know that playing coy will get you nowhere with me,' she returned wryly with a touch of exasperation. 'I'm the forthright Harriet Wiley, remember? Do you really think I don't know you'd rather go to bed with Ty than fight with him?'

The breath rushed out of Revel's lungs. '*Hattie*!' she exclaimed in mortified shock, crimsoning.

'Well, I'm right, aren't I?'

Revel couldn't answer. She could only move her head helplessly, remembering that going to bed with Ty had been exactly her wish only a week ago.

'I know I would, if I were in your shoes,' Hattie now added whimsically in her own inimitable fashion, and Revel's involuntary half-laugh in response caught on something close to a sob.

'Oh, Hattie, what am I going to do?' she cried strickenly.

The older woman touched a comforting hand to her still moist cheek, and then brushed aside the ragged fringe from her forehead in a maternal gesture. 'Stay and work it out would appear the most logical, don't you think?' she proposed on a soothing note. 'As I seem to recollect suggesting when you first arrived, why not try a little communication instead of only confrontation?'

Tyler had also said something similar, Revel recalled, but, of course, that had been before today. She drew a shivering breath. 'I somehow doubt he'd be interested,' she put forward miserably. 'You saw what he was like downstairs.' Her voice began to rise as she twisted her fingers together tightly. 'Well, it was even worse out there this afternoon, Hattie. He really looked at me as if I were his enemy!'

'And would that have been before, or after, your— um—unfortunate comment to the media?' The older woman's mouth shaped ruefully.

Revel caught at her soft lower lip with shining white teeth. 'After, I guess,' she owned on a dismal note, the image in her mind's eye having been that of Tyler's glance as the police van departed. Then, with more than a tinge of resentment, 'Not that he was much less grim beforehand, in any case.'

'No, I don't suppose he was,' Hattie acceded sympathetically. 'Being plain-dealing himself, Ty values honesty above most things.'

Revel's eyes widened in dismay. 'You're saying you don't believe I had nothing to do with the demonstrators being there either?' she gasped. 'But I didn't tell them where Ty's men were working, Hattie. I swear I didn't!'

'And I believe you.' The other woman's reassurance came swiftly as she laid a hand on Revel's tightly entwined fingers. 'Where Ty's concerned, however...' She exhaled heavily. 'Unfortunately I don't think you realise just how hard he took your little deception when you first arrived.'

As it had turned out, Revel could only agree—now. 'A point which would simply seem to make it all the more advisable that I leave,' she declared with a sigh. 'Moreover, there is still the matter of the credibility factor, should it be discovered I'm living here, anyway.'

Hattie shrugged. 'You don't think that's our worry rather than yours? Besides, your being here has always carried the same risk, even before today's appearance on TV, but since it hasn't been discovered to date...' She paused, tilting her head to one side. 'Anyhow, if you do still really believe there's reason to protest, surely you should be envisaging any such chance of furthering your cause with satisfaction, not concern,' she suggested slyly, which brought a despondent grimace to Revel's face.

'Except that I'm none too certain I know just what to believe any more,' she confessed moodily.

'Then, as I said, you'd better stay until you find out,' Hattie stated in her most decisive tone, and Revel expelled a long breath.

'But—but what about Mr Corrigan and—Ty?' She swallowed. 'How can I stay when they must surely——?'

'Or maybe they're just hoping that one of these days you'll stop demonstrating, and start discussing,' came the wryly voiced insertion. 'Because every tree felled is not automatically an environmental disaster...as the untested claims of your fringe group would have people believe.' She held up an arresting hand when Revel would have spoken. 'No one, and least of all us, denies we need to protect and conserve our forests to the very best of our ability, but, by the same token, nor can we afford to forgo all progress by declining to make the most of those assets we have. It merely risks having to reduce human endeavour to levels incapable of sustaining our present standards of living.' She quirked an expressive brow. 'And that, I'd hazard a guess to say, is very definitely not what the less vocal *majority*——' pointedly stressed '—of people want.'

Revel chewed at the inside of her lip thoughtfully, remembering how, on that first Sunday with Tyler, she herself had decried the idea of returning to such primitive lifestyles. Nevertheless...

'Even so, Ty still admitted there were areas in his op-
eration that needed to be bettered,' she relayed with just
a hint of satisfaction.

'Quite possibly.' The other woman's ready willingness
to concede the point took a little of the wind out of
Revel's sails. 'As much as it may surprise you, loggers
and caring for the environment are not mutually ex-
clusive,' she declared drily. 'Ty's always looking for ways
to reduce the effects of logging to the barest minimum.'
She smiled and patted Revel on the knee. 'And now that's
settled, I think it's time you had your dinner. I brought
it up with me——' beginning to gain her feet, and indicating on the bedside table a covered tray which Revel
only then noticed '—and I'm sure you must be famished
after all this time.' She peered under the cover with a
frown. 'Although I suppose it could need re-heating by
now.'

'No, please don't bother,' Revel vetoed when it seemed
as if Hattie meant to take the tray downstairs again. 'It
was very thoughtful of you to bring it in the first place.'
She paused, her gaze turning apologetic. 'And I'm afraid
I don't really feel much like eating, anyway.'

'As long as you make certain you have *some*.' It was
a command, not a request, which earned an acquiescent
nod along with the glimmerings of a weak half-smile.
In response Hattie tilted Revel's tear-stained face upwards with a hand cupping her chin. 'Meanwhile, just
keep in mind that Tyler would doubtlessly rather make
love to you than fight with you, too.' She was back to
her most plain-spoken again. 'I've never known any
female have such an effect on him as you did when you
first arrived,' she added with a fondly reassuring smile,
and made her exit.

Alone once more, Revel hardly knew what to think.
The only fact of which she was certain was that it appeared she would be staying—again!

CHAPTER TEN

'OH, REVEL, how could you?'

It was mid-morning the following day when Isabel Ballard, along with Revel's brother, Quentin, arrived without warning at the house, her first words on sighting her daughter duplicating Hattie's of the previous evening as her mother's friend led the two visitors through to the comfortably appointed family room.

'And after Hattie and Ellis have apparently been kind enough to allow you to stay here, too!' Isabel continued chidingly as she gave her daughter a distracted kiss, and allowing Revel no time to do more than smile at her brother in acknowledgement of his presence. 'I can't begin to tell you what your father had to say about the matter. Surely you must have known how he—we——' a fluttering hand included Quentin and herself '—would feel having the Ballard name dragged to the fore of something so radical and in such a *deplorable* manner. Have you no consideration for your family any more since meeting up with these—these revolutionaries?' She subsided on to the sofa behind her with a little moan, and looking faint.

Revel didn't have to ask just what had put her parent into such a distraught state. She might not have seen the TV coverage of the previous afternoon's events herself, but it was becoming more than obvious that she must have figured prominently and her impulsive statement used to great effect.

None the less, she still had no compunction in contradicting wryly, 'Wanting to protect the environment doesn't necessarily make you a revolutionary, Mum.' She sent an eloquent glance in her brother's direction as they also seated themselves. Only, to her surprise, in response it merely received the barest semblance of the usual smile she had been anticipating. 'And I'm sorry if what you evidently saw on the TV upset you,' she went on, returning her attention to her mother. 'Actually, I've been doing my best *not* to appear on camera.'

'Then with little success, it would appear, unfortunately, since we've also seen you helping to form human chains across roads, mounting blockades, and goodness knows what else,' Quentin now entered the conversation to impart with an ironic and slightly disapproving air. 'Yesterday just happened to be the last straw, what with you clambering over equipment, then that shamefully maudlin scene with the tears, and, just to cap it all off, a lingering shot of you struggling as you were being thrust into a police van!' He heaved an exasperated breath. 'Good lord, have you any idea just how many phone calls Dad and I had to parry last night as a result of all that?'

Revel's fingers tightened on the arm of the sofa she was sitting on. 'I've already said I'm sorry!' she flared, assailed by feelings of guilt at his revelations, yet at the same time just a touch rebellious as well. After the night before, more condemnation was the last thing she was in the mood to suffer. 'Or was it just the fact that your dignity was ruffled by all those phone calls that's brought you racing up here?'

'Is that what you think?' he demanded, sitting forward, and suddenly looking more wrathful than she could remember. 'Well, it certainly appears as if I have a higher regard for my sister than she does for me, because it was purely concern for you that brought me "racing up here", as you put it! I admit I could have done without the questions and implications your little antics have already raised, but it was worry over you, and what you were allowing yourself to be pushed into, that had us deciding to come here.'

'After all, you did say you weren't planning on doing anything outlandish, Revel,' her mother reminded reproachfully. 'You just wanted to see for yourself what was happening, you said.' Her gaze turned even more hurt. 'You also promised you would give me a ring to let me know how you were. And when I find you're even staying with Hattie and didn't let me know...' She expelled an expressive breath.

Revel looked away discomfitedly. Oh, hell, she'd forgotten all about ringing her mother, what with everything that had happened. 'I'm sorry. I just didn't think,' she apologised in a sighing voice. She slanted an abashed glance at her brother. 'And I'm sorry for what I said to you, too, Quentin. It's just that...well, the last twenty-four hours have been somewhat trying.' Not the least of it caused by the fact that she hadn't yet seen Tyler that morning, she acknowledged apprehensively. He had already left the house when she came downstairs and she was on tenterhooks as to exactly what his attitude might be when they next met. She hurried on, hoping to divert their attention from the previous day's events. 'So you weren't expecting to see me here when you arrived?'

'Well, of course not. We had absolutely no idea where you were,' Isabel returned a little huffily. 'When our enquiries elicited Hattie's address, naturally we came here first. Apart from my wishing to see her, anyway, we could only hope that you had at least kept one of your promises and come to see her, with the result that she might know where we could find you.'

'And thereby managed to kill two birds with one stone,' quipped Revel with simulated brightness in an attempt to relieve the strained atmosphere.

Isabel was obviously of another mind, for she promptly reproved, 'Now is not the time for flippancy, Revel! I'm extremely disappointed in you. And not only

because of your behaviour yesterday either. I mean to
say, how could you—*how could you*——' her voice
thinned with indignation '—have been so discourteous
and ungrateful as to demonstrate against logging while
living under Ellis Corrigan's roof?'

Revel gave a diffident shrug, and instinctively answered
with a protective glibness once more. 'Although not while
I was actually under his roof. Hattie wouldn't counten-
ance any dissension in the house.'

Her mother's face took on a pained look. 'Revel, this
is not a joking matter,' she said faintly, putting a hand
to her brow. 'It's appalling enough, you accepting Ellis's
hospitality while participating in a protest against him,
but to then accuse him on national TV of—of unjustified abuse of the forest . . . well, it's just totally beyond
the bounds of what's acceptable.'

'Except that it wasn't Mr Corrigan I was accusing, it
was his son.'

'Revel!' Quentin now added his own remonstrance,
but it was their mother who continued it.

'Now you're merely quibbling,' she charged in her
most vexed tone. 'And it has no bearing whether it was
Ellis or his son, in any event. I just don't know what
you can have been thinking of. Your behaviour has been
totally incomprehensible, not to mention a most
thoughtless embarrassment to both——'

'What, you still in strife, lass?' an amiable male voice
suddenly intervened from the doorway and, looking
round self-consciously, Revel found Ellis Corrigan, with
Tyler following, just entering the room. With her back
to the door and listening to her mother's outpouring,
she hadn't noticed the return of their vehicle, and she
flushed at having been discovered being taken to task
again. 'Give the kid a break, Isabel,' the older man continued, ruffling Revel's hair as he passed her. 'She copped
a fair blast last night, and it's not a day to be getting
all hot and bothered.'

'Yes, give it a rest, Isabel,' added Hattie on returning to the room with a laden tray after having previously departed to prepare some morning tea. 'I could hear you from the kitchen. You haven't let up on the girl since you arrived.' Placing the tray on the table, she smiled at Ellis. 'I'll need another couple of cups now that you're back.' She turned for the kitchen again.

'Besides, this is the first time I've seen you in years, and we don't want to waste the time crying over spilt milk,' Ellis went on inhibitingly when it seemed as if Isabel was about to splutter into piqued speech once more. 'So how's life been treating you in the big smoke? And this must be Quentin, I presume?' He smiled and offered an outstretched hand to that man, who had already risen to his feet. 'Revel's often mentioned you.'

His words instigated the other introductions that also needed to be made, and by the time they were completed Revel was thankful to note that her mother's attention appeared to have been diverted—at least for the time being—along less contentious avenues than that of her daughter's behaviour.

What she wasn't so thankful about were the subsequent seating arrangements. Hattie returned to settle herself beside Isabel, while Quentin resumed his previous seat, and Ellis lowered himself into his usual chair. That left only one vacant position—next to herself—and when Tyler made use of it she could feel her every nerve tensing.

Admittedly, he had been pleasant enough when greeting her mother and brother, but just what could she expect when it came to herself?

A surreptitious sidelong glance from beneath the screen of her lashes revealed his expression to be remote, inaccessible, and for some unknown reason that caused her even more concern than she suspected continuing anger would have done. At least when he was angry he wasn't detached from her. Although why the thought of being disregarded by him should have occasioned such a dispiriting feeling, she didn't stop to analyse. She merely acted spontaneously to bridge the gulf that seemed to be widening between them.

'Ty,' she murmured tentatively under cover of the others' voices as they flowed around them while Hattie dispensed the cups of tea, and putting out a tentative hand towards him, 'I truly am sorry for what happened yesterday.'

For a moment Revel was uncertain whether he had heard, or simply didn't mean to answer. But then he slowly turned his head the merest fraction to view her from the corners of his eyes.

'Why?' he countered flatly, and her brows drew together in a doubtful frown.

'Why—am I sorry?' She moved her shoulders deprecatorily. 'Well—I—it really wasn't my intention to cause added trouble for you and your father.'

One corner of his mouth pulled in imperceptibly, but when he spoke his tone remained expressionless. 'You mean, by divulging our whereabouts, or as a result of your emotional declaration?'

Revel pressed her lips together. 'I meant the latter, of course . . . since, as I kept telling you, I had no hand in the former,' she all but gritted, struggling to remember to keep her voice down.

Tyler merely gave a shake of his head. But to her surprise the action seemed more confounded than dismissive. 'Well, whichever, I'm afraid your brand of logic still escapes me.'

'Logic?' Bewilderment edged across her lightly flushed features. 'I don't understand.'

For the first time a trace of emotion—impatience?— flashed in his eyes, and then just as quickly disappeared again. 'Then if it's not your intention to cause us trouble, perhaps you would care to explain just why in hell you're demonstrating against us?' he proposed on a heavily released breath.

Revel swallowed, remembering Hattie's remark of the previous evening, which basically had been in a similar vein, not to mention her own disconcerting thoughts on feeling as if she had somehow betrayed him.

'I'm only trying to do what—seems right,' she put forward disconsolately.

'To you . . . or them?'

'Why can't it be both?'

'I thought you'd already made that distinction yourself, when you warned us they were likely to pay the mill a visit.'

Revel shifted uncomfortably, reluctantly recalling other words and actions that had also raised certain misgivings within her. 'Yes—but——'

'And why on earth, out of all the groups to choose from, would you align yourself with that band of maverick militants?' he broke in to question.

Revel shrugged. 'I attended their meetings, and——'

'Fell for their tear-jerking slogans,' Tyler finished for her with his own interpretation, shaking his head in disbelief. 'So what were they this time? That we're running out resources and the forest here will be cut to extinction within a decade?'

'Three years,' she amended swiftly, and he lifted a dark brow.

'Only three now? My, they must getting desperate for new supporters.' Pausing, he regarded her curiously. 'But tell me, now that you've seen the forest for yourself, and spent some time up there, do you honestly believe it will have disappeared within three years?'

Revel's gaze automatically sought the tree-clad hills that were visible through the window behind Ellis Corrigan. 'Well—no,' she had to allow, moistening her lips. 'But then, as you well know, I've never claimed to

be an expert on the subject either,' honesty also compelled her to qualify.

'Although you didn't let that stop you from hot-
footing it up here from your de-forested city in order to
show us poor, unperceptive country simpletons the error
of our ways with the benefit of that almost non-existent
knowledge.' A definite trace of sarcasm made an appearance, and Revel felt the heat of a flush suffuse her
cheeks. 'And that, presumably, despite the fact that in
democracies it's usual to require proof—irrefutable,
authoritative *proof*—before making such far-reaching
judgements.'

'Sebastian says he has proof,' she retorted defensively, and, because her voice had been louder than she
intended, immediately darted a swift look around the
room to see if she had inadvertently attracted any unwanted attention. She was relieved to note, however, that
the others' conversation continued without pause. The
three older occupants of the room were obviously making
the most of their reunion.

'And you've seen this—documented—so-called evidence?' Tyler now probed sceptically.

Revel bent her head. 'Not exactly.'

'Meaning?'

'All right! No, I haven't seen it,' she conceded on a
flaring note, and suddenly found herself wondering if
she had a hitherto unrecognised streak of perverseness
somewhere in her nature. As always, when she was with
Tyler she defended Sebastian, and when she was with
the other man she ended up doing the reverse.

'Yet you continue to believe him when he claims there's
a need to protest,' Tyler mused. He ran a hand around
the back of his neck wearily. 'I just don't understand
you. Unless, of course——' his gaze sharpened fractionally '—your personal involvement with him is deeper
than you're revealing.'

Implying, once again, that she was deceiving him about that as well, she supposed indignantly. 'Except that there never really has been a personal relationship between us,' she retorted peremptorily. There might have been the chance for one once, but not since she had met Tyler. Besides, wasn't it only a week ago that she had been in his own arms? Or did he really believe that her emotions were that capricious? A hollow feeling formed in the pit of her stomach at the thought, even as she added for good measure, if a touch resentfully, 'Moreover, I'm not sure he's even my type. I find his perpetual fervency and——'

'Extremism?' he put in insinuatingly, and Revel's lips compressed in vexation.

'It is not extreme to want to protect the environment, Tyler,' she denounced tautly.

That did bring about a definite reaction. An unequivocally derogatory snort, to her chagrin. 'It is when the objectives are to halt, without exception, *all* logging . . . and mining, and industry, and farming on a commercial basis! What's more, you do realise, I presume, that another of their ambitions is not only to prevent any new water-storage dams being built—irrespective of the needs of an increasing population—but also to have demolished all those already constructed, in order that nature might once again determine the flow, or otherwise, of all waterways?' he submitted in satirical accents.

Revel's chin promptly lifted. 'And I've only your word for it that those are their aims! Certainly no mention of any such objectives has ever been made in my hearing.'

'"In your hearing" being the operative words, of course! But if it's confirmation you want, why not ask your own brother?' Tyler took her aback by unexpectedly advocating. 'If he's as involved in politics as you mentioned, I'll be surprised if he's not already well aware of your little group, and their true ambitions.' He paused, a provokingly goading look entering his eyes. 'Or you could even try questioning Renwick himself...*if* you're game enough to hear the answers, and he's willing to provide them truthfully.'

'Don't worry, I intend to,' she was impelled into declaring heatedly. 'And "game" has nothing to do with it. I simply think he has the right to defend himself against *your* claims, that's all.'

'How very charitable of you,' Tyler was swift to quip, with a bite. 'It's more than you ever accorded us before you started demonstrating.' And, in a disdainfully dismissive gesture, he turned away from her to deliberately enter the others' conversation.

Even without his scrutiny, however, Revel still had the grace to blush, knowing that his charge wasn't one she could deny, and her discomfiture made all the worse through the knowledge of her own increasing misgivings concerning Sebastian's own actions involving herself...and, by no means least, by her awareness that his original call for logging in the State forests to be halted had, indeed, of late merely become a cry for halting logging...period.

In the meantime, and not altogether surprisingly, she supposed with a sigh, it appeared that she was no closer to resolving her differences with Ty than she had been before he sat down. So, if he wanted to ignore her, why should she let it concern her? she tried telling herself bracingly. In fact, two could play at that game. Yet it was to Ty that her eyes constantly strayed as the weekend progressed.

It was Monday before Revel managed to see Sebastian again, and even then she had difficulty in keeping him in one place long enough to receive answers to the questions that had been niggling at her with such increasing insistence. The more so after a talk with her brother had

elicited much the same comments as Tyler's regarding
the group.

'Questions? What sort of questions?' Sebastian countered with a shortness born of distraction at her first
mention of any such queries, his attention and efforts
all concentrated on mustering the protesters towards the
vehicles, and hurriedly since the weather had taken a
turn for the worse again. There was a strong, cold wind
blowing, the sky grey and heavy and an indication of
the amount of rain that was just starting to fall. 'I haven't
the time for that now. You'll have to wait until we're on
our way, or when we reach block ten. We've had our
scouts out all weekend and we're pretty sure we've found
where they'll be logging this morning,' he concluded on
a victorious note.

'Oh, but...' Revel faltered to a halt, hanging back a
little. Without the answers she was seeking, she was
averse to taking part in any such likely confrontation
again, and especially if Tyler happened to be present.
'Er—actually, I would have preferred to talk to you
alone,' she relayed awkwardly.

That did at least succeed in stopping him, if only momentarily, as he turned to stare at her intently, his brows
lowering in a frown. 'Then it will definitely have to be
later,' he dismissed with a shrug as he pulled open the
door of the Land Rover next to them. Almost immediately he sang out to the others, 'Come on, everyone,
let's get moving!' And in the resultant rush to fill the
available vehicles Revel found herself jostled unceremoniously into the Land Rover along with the rest of
them.

As on her first day, Revel could at least be grateful
for the extra warmth provided inside the vehicle, and the
fact that on this occasion she was more suitably attired—even if the colours of her clothes weren't exactly
becoming!

The trail they followed was also one that she didn't remember travelling before, and seemed to lead deeper into the forest than any of the others, so that after a while she completely lost track of the direction in which they were heading as the trees appeared to close in more thickly and darkly around them.

'This is virgin forest! It's never been logged before!' exclaimed the girl in the front seat next to Sebastian.

'Yes! We've got to put paid to their cutting this,' agreed someone else.

Then, suddenly, the noise of chain-saws could be heard, and shortly thereafter they came across some of the loggers' machinery, including Tyler's ute, Revel noted with a sinking feeling. Within minutes the vehicles braked to a stop, their occupants hurrying eagerly into the rain.

Waiting only long enough to ensure that the scene was captured by the ever-present TV crews, Sebastian promptly ordered, 'All right, everybody...scatter! They'll have to stop if there's the risk of someone being injured—or worse.'

Whooping and yelling figures immediately began racing among the trees in all directions, although Revel made no move to join them, but remained, undecided, beside the Land Rover. At least, that was until Sebastian chanced to look back before disappearing from sight and happened to see her there.

'What are you waiting for...the police to arrive?' he shouted impatiently. 'You're coming, too, aren't you?' His mouth pulled downwards. 'You'll have to, if you want to ask me anything.'

Without even waiting for an answer, he continued on into the bush, and, of necessity, it seemed as if Revel had no option but to follow him. Since Ty hadn't yet made an appearance, it might be better if he didn't know she was there, she consoled herself as she started tramping through the dripping undergrowth.

Ahead of her came the sound of voices raised in argument, and, guessing that it indicated the loggers' realisation of the protesters' presence, Revel altered course to avoid the area—just in case Tyler was involved—and hastened on her way, deeper into the forest.

The number of chain-saws seemed to be decreasing now, she noticed absently, and then all at once her ears picked up a noise—a cracking, splintering, ominous noise which she had only ever heard before in movies or on TV—that had her blood running cold and her heart lurching to a halt. A tree was coming down—near by! she realised in something akin to panic, her eyes swiftly lifting skywards to see a crown of branches rushing towards her.

Thankfully fear lent her feet wings, although to Revel it seemed as if she moved agonisingly slowly, and she literally threw herself out of the tree's path behind the protective bulk of another of its kind. Even so, as it slammed to the ground in a jolting, crashing thud, she felt the sting of one its outermost branches as the tip whipped across her cheek and shoulder, cutting both her skin and her parka in the process.

Ashen-faced at such a close call, Revel could only remain sprawled where she was for a moment or two, waiting for her nerves to stop quivering. Then, hearing the approaching footsteps of the feller as he prepared to start trimming the tree, she somehow found the strength to scramble to her feet in order to flee. When she first appeared from behind the tree, however, the man's own features promptly lost almost as much colour as her own on observing her appearance, and he let fly with a string of extremely explicit epithets.

'You bloody brainless bitch! Get the hell out of here!' he went on to roar in a mixture of fury and shock as she took to her heels. 'You could have been bloody killed!'

He thought he needed to tell *her* that! Revel gulped near-hysterically, and was still attempting to regain some measure of control over her madly racing pulse when she stumbled upon Sebastian near the weathered stump of a previously felled tree. Which eliminated the idea that it was virgin forest, at least, she recognised inconsequentially.

'What on earth happened to you?' Sebastian immediately exclaimed, eyeing her muddied and dishevelled clothing askance. 'Did you fall over, or something?'

'More like something almost fell over me,' she felt sufficiently recovered to quip, shakily, as she tried to rid herself of the wet leaves splattered over her clothing.

'You mean, you were nearly caught by a falling tree?' His voice started to rise, and Revel could only wonder if she was doing him an injustice by thinking the nuance she detected was one of excited satisfaction. 'Quick, we'd better return to the track, then, so we can show everyone the proof of the dangers involved if they continue felling,' he proposed urgently, and already beginning to urge her back the way she had come. 'No, don't wipe it away,' he added in veto when she put a hand to her still smarting cheek and her fingers came away stained with blood—albeit watery blood, due to the rain. 'Let everyone see the effects of what happens when it comes down to a contest between the rights of people and the callous pursuit of profit. That's your badge of honour!'

Revel was more inclined to suspect that it was simply another fortuitous opportunity for *him* to capture extra media coverage, but forbore from saying so. She had other points to dispute, in any case.

'The effects of a contest!' She just couldn't hold back the incredulous expostulation any longer as she determinedly came to a halt. 'If anyone's to blame, I am, for being in a restricted area in the first place! And, what's more, I have no intention of parading the result of my irresponsible action for all the world to see.' And that was quite apart from the fact that she was still suffering the consequences of her last indiscriminate TV appearance!

'Irresponsible? What do you mean—irresponsible?' it was Sebastian's turn to repeat disbelievingly now. 'We do what we have to, to ensure logging's brought to a halt. How else are we to achieve our long-term aims?'

'Yes—well—that was actually what I was wanting to talk to you about,' Revel gratefully accepted the opportunity to disclose. Her head tilted enquiringly. 'So just exactly what are your long-term aims, Sebastian?'

Briefly his expression became veiled, and then he shrugged. 'To show society we have to become less materialistic and consumer-orientated, and more dedicated to higher causes.'

'Such as?'

'Living at one with nature, banning exploitative development . . . and returning the land to all the people, not just allowing the few to work it for their own personal benefit!' An impassioned and rather bitter note entered his voice at the last. 'It's time we stopped using our natural resources for mere profit, and returned to a more fundamental and unpretentious way of life.'

Just as Tyler, and Quentin, had claimed? Revel speculated with a sigh. Although she did also wonder if there hadn't been a hint of sour grapes in there as well. Nevertheless, her succeeding efforts in seeking further elucidation, she discovered to be more informative for what Sebastian didn't—or wouldn't—reveal than for what he did. So much so, in fact, that in the end the atmosphere was decidedly tense between them, and it was only the sudden appearance of a distinctively blue-uniformed male that managed to relieve it.

'Well, I'm off,' Sebastian said hastily—and not a little gratefully, surmised Revel—on sighting the police officer, and without a backward glance rapidly suited his action to his words.

Scant seconds later Revel was also making herself scarce in another direction. Despite already having made up her mind to return to the track—but for her own reasons—she still had not the slightest desire to be escorted there in the custody of the law. She would simply circle around him and make her own way back, she decided.

However, by the time she had concluded her evasive peregrinations, the rain was not only bucketing down but she was hopelessly lost as well, Revel realised in mounting dismay. On top of which, just to make it even less pleasant, the rip in her parka was now admitting so much water that her jumper was quickly becoming as wet as her jeans and trainers, and she was beginning to shiver with the cold as well.

It was turning into nothing more than a disastrous repeat of her very first day! she lamented in despairing vexation.

CHAPTER ELEVEN

IT SEEMED like hours—she had no doubts that it *was* hours—before Revel finally managed to locate a snigging track, but whether it was the same one they had used earlier, she had no idea. Certainly there was no sign of any vehicles, and nothing looked in the least familiar.

Actually, she had been a little surprised that in all her tramping she hadn't come across any of the other protesters. Perhaps they had called the action off due to the weather, or she had simply wandered too far away from them, she'd had to conclude.

Now, as she tossed up mentally as to which way to go, she decided that, since she hadn't a clue which was the right direction, she might as well take the easier-going—downhill—and set off accordingly. Then suddenly, another miserably plodded half-mile further on, some sixth sense must have alerted her, sending her gaze swinging towards the trees beside the track and her heart leaping into her throat on seeing a tall male figure in the shadows.

Clad in a full-length, dark brown oilskin coat with caped shoulders, his head covered by a broad-brimmed bush hat, it seemed almost as if he had been waiting for her as he leant negligently against the trunk of the tree that, together with the brim of his hat and the still pouring rain, kept his features obscured.

'Ty...?' Revel breathed unsteadily, instinct telling her his identity despite the note of enquiry in her voice.

Pushing away from the tree, he gave the briefest of nods, and she felt her knees come close to buckling in relief at the knowledge that she wasn't lost any more. The prospect of perhaps having to spend the night in the forest as well had been more than a little daunting.

169

'Wh-what are you doing here?' she stammered, shivering, and feeling the cold even more now that she'd stopped moving.

'What do you think I'm doing here?' His mouth shaped ironically.

Revel swallowed. 'You were—looking for me?'

'Well, I'm not here for my health, I can assure you.' One eyebrow arched expressively. 'Or do you know someone else who also regularly gets themselves lost up here?'

Although not considering his 'regularly' to be strictly fair, Revel wasn't about to dispute it in the circumstances. 'But how did you know where to look, or even that I was lost, if it comes to that?'

Tyler shrugged. 'Regarding the latter, certain events made it likely. While as for the former, once I'd checked block ten, with no result, I *didn't* know where you were. That's why it's taken me over two hours!' he heaved in roughened tones. 'Did you have to wander quite so far from where you started?'

Revel bit at her lip and answered with apologetic honesty, 'I didn't know I had. It all looks the same to me.'

Tyler's ensuing expression was explicit. 'Then it might have been better if you'd stayed out of it to begin with.'

'I would have done, if I'd had the choice,' she asserted, and he gave a sharp shake of his head in negation.

'Oh, spare me the claims of it not having been your intention,' he scorned. 'I've heard them all before.'

Revel's head lifted as resentment flared. 'Then if that's how you feel, why bother to look for me at all?' Pausing, she grimaced eloquently. 'No, you don't have to tell me, I already know why. To avoid giving you even more reason to regret my coming by expiring on your doorstep,' she quoted the words he'd used the night her car had become bogged.

'In which case, we'd better get moving, before you do precisely that,' he showed no aversion to suggesting. 'It's a pity you don't show the same concern for your own welfare as you do for that of the trees.' He expelled a heavy breath and gestured with his head towards the trees behind him. 'Come on—this way.'

Revel's eyes widened. 'Not down there?' she quizzed, indicating the track even as she moved away from it. She had wondered why he'd made no move to join her.

Tyler shook his head. 'Uh-uh, it's a dead end that way. You were heading in the wrong direction if you were hoping to connect with another road, and the ute's on a completely different track, anyhow.'

Sighing ruefully, Revel nodded. Heading in the wrong direction or into dead ends seemed to have become the story of her life since arriving at Mount Winsome! Then all such thoughts abruptly vanished when, on reaching Tyler, he startled her by suddenly catching hold of her chin and tilting upwards her cut cheek, which had been turned away from him before.

'It *was* you!' he exclaimed in a rasping voice. 'I thought it had to be, from Jay's description.' He made an exasperated movement with his head. 'You damned idiot! What were you trying to do...commit suicide? You frightened ten years off Jay's life with that fool stunt, especially when he saw blood on your face.'

Revel shivered, both with the cold and at the memory of the incident. 'I strongly suspect it took a few years off m-my life, too,' she quipped unsteadily and, seeing her shaken state, Tyler's expression softened marginally.

'Does it still hurt?' he murmured, touching a thumb softly to the mark, washed clean by the rain now, and all at once she found it difficult to breathe.

'N-not as much as it did,' she supplied in a throaty whisper, her eyes locking with his, the pouring rain forgotten. A shivery sensation swept through her as she involuntarily recalled the feel and taste of his lips on hers, the strength of his sinewed arms holding her securely close. And suddenly she was wishing he would kiss her now; wishing everything was as it had been between them in the beginning; wishing he loved her as much as she realised abruptly that she had come to love him! And for a brief second, as his head appeared to lower, she believed that he was going to kiss her. But then, to her despair, he straightened tautly and took a step backwards, making her flush with mortification at the thought that he might have been aware of her desire and wanted nothing to do with it.

'And hell, you're also frozen again,' he observed on a newly harsh note. 'I'm starting to think you need a keeper.'

Revel bent her head. Not because she accepted his assessment, but in order to gain time in which to cloak her lacerated feelings. Simultaneously, however, she was also very much aware that if he had cared to apply for such a position she would have welcomed it.

Aloud, she merely offered in a small voice, 'The tree tore my parka, which then let the water in.' She hunched one shoulder diffidently. 'Not that I think it would have withstood this downpour for so long, in any event.'

'Then in the name of heaven why didn't you remain in the vicinity of the rest of them?' Tyler demanded. 'They returned to the camp hours ago.'

'Because I'd already decided to take no further part and was trying to find my way back to the vehicles.' Curiosity had her looking up at last, and probing with a frown, 'But how do you know they returned to camp, anyway?'

'Because I saw them as I was leaving,' he relayed impassively as he started off through the underbrush with a lithe, ground-covering stride.

'The camp?' Revel began to doubt her ears. 'You went to the camp?' she gasped, hurrying to keep up with him. Just what the reaction to such a visit might have been, she couldn't even begin to hazard a guess.

'It seemed the most logical place to make enquiries as to your whereabouts when you hadn't returned to the house two hours after we'd packed up for the day,' he advised flatly. 'There wasn't much to be gained in your remaining out there once we'd left.'

Revel could see his point. 'And did they recognise you?' she quizzed a trifle apprehensively. Talk about laying one's head on the line!

Tyler flexed an indifferent shoulder. 'I didn't ask.' He flashed her a sardonic glance. 'The place wasn't exactly a hive of activity, and the woman I spoke to was more interested in keeping out of the rain than in discovering who I was.' A faint pause. 'Which must be a relief to you, I'm sure.'

Surprise had Revel forgetting to look where she was going so that it was only on regaining her balance, after tripping over an exposed root, that she was able to puzzle, 'A relief? Why?'

Tyler slanted her a speaking look, his mouth levelling. 'Obviously because it relieves you of the embarrassing necessity to explain why a Corrigan—one of the odious logging fraternity—would be asking for you.'

It was the perfect opportunity for Revel to tell him that she didn't intend associating with Sebastian and his group any more, but before she could do so she stumbled again, this time almost falling to her knees, and the chance was lost as Tyler came to an exasperated halt.

'For crying out loud, we're never going to get anywhere if you can't keep on your feet for more than two steps at a time,' he growled, and most unfairly, to her mind.

'I can't help it!' she promptly fired back in reproachful accents. 'My feet are so cold, I can't feel whether my footing's secure or not.'

Tyler muttered something under his breath and, before Revel knew it, she had been swept off her frozen feet into his arms and he was continuing on his way with that long-striding pace of his.

'But you can't carry me all the way,' she demurred once she had recovered from the shock of his solution to the problem.

'I seem to be making a better fist of it than you were,' came the indisputable reply, and, because she actually found herself anything but averse to the position she was in, Revel linked her arms about the strong column of his neck and rested her head against his shoulder acquiescently.

Whether he wanted it or not, she liked being this close to him, and so were her legs appreciative of the respite from all the walking they had done so far that day. In fact, the only really discomfiting aspect was the way the water kept dripping from the brim of his hat on to her head, although why it should have made itself felt so noticeably amid all the rain that was still falling on them, Revel wasn't certain. She just knew that it did and, in consequence, ventured to shift the angle of his head-covering so that the water was directed elsewhere.

'You're positive that's quite satisfactory to you?' Tyler immediately looked down at her to quip in gruff tones as all the water now began to spill on to his opposite shoulder, and Revel couldn't restrain the twitch that caught at her lips.

'Well, I was sure you wouldn't wish to add to the soaking I've already received,' she excused with a dubious degree of meekness.

'Hmm. You do squelch, at that,' he declared repressively, and which, she supposed, was an apt description, if not a particularly flattering one.

Moreover, now that once again she wasn't generating extra body heat by walking, the cold was beginning to bite more deeply and making her shiver uncontrollably despite her instinctively burrowing closer to Tyler in search of the warmth that she could feel emanating from him even through the layers of their clothing.

As a result, she could only be thankful when at last the ute loomed into view through the grey curtain of the rain, and heave an even more grateful sigh when they were ensconced within its sheltering interior.

'Here, take your jacket off and put this on,' Tyler directed urgently, tossing her a tartan woollen rug that had been on the back shelf, and turning the key in the ignition in order to set the heater going at full strength. 'You look about ready to pass out. Oh, and you'd better give me your feet as well.'

'My f-feet?' Revel stuttered, teeth chattering, and her numbed fingers stopping their attempt to undo the top fastener of her parka.

'Mmm, a rub will get your circulation moving again quicker than by the warmth from the heater only,' he proposed briskly, his own hands taking over from hers and deftly peeling her sodden jacket from her in next to no time. No sooner had her equally saturated sweater been exposed, though, than he was exclaiming, 'Hell, there's no point in wrapping a rug over that! Come on, lift your arms, and we'll get rid of this, too!' His fingers took hold of the lower edge of the soggy garment.

'No!' Revel protested with a gulp, the first trace of colour returning to her face as she determinedly kept her arms at her sides. 'No, really, it's n-not necessary. I dare say I'll survive until we r-reach——'

'And if you were seated where I am you might not be so certain of that,' Tyler interjected roughly. 'So forget about being bashful and just do as you're told, hmm?' His expression assumed an ironic cast. 'After all, it's not exactly as if I haven't seen you wearing less previously.'

A reminder that did nothing to ease Revel's self-consciousness, but before she could object further he was already dragging her sweater upwards, his sheer strength raising her arms along with it. He was also the one eventually to wrap her snugly in the soft tartan wool, her own still somewhat benumbed limbs apparently not functioning either swiftly or ably enough for his liking.

'Well, isn't that better?' he demanded, proceeding to give his attention to unceremoniously tugging her trainers and socks from her feet now, and, with the added warmth from the heater decidedly starting to make itself felt, Revel could only nod in agreement.

'And thank you for that, too,' she said softly a short time later after he had patiently rubbed some feeling back into her feet. She gave a rueful little smile. 'That's the first time they've been warm since it started to rain this morning.'

Although he stopped rubbing Tyler didn't remove his hands from the foot he had last been attending to, and Revel was increasingly aware of the fact. 'I guess it hasn't really been one of your better days, has it?' he mused with unexpected gentleness. She had half anticipated being told that she only had herself to blame.

'No, very definitely no,' she was encouraged to agree with an eloquent grimace. 'Although I wasn't the only one, apparently. By the sound of the thumping I heard during my wanderings there must have been at least a couple of other creatures having a spot of trouble as well.'

'Thumping?' A frown appeared between Tyler's brows.

'Well, more a series of thuds, really. Not that I ever saw or found anything when I went to investigate, though.' She shrugged dismissively.

Not so Tyler. All of a sudden he seemed to tense like a coiled spring, a hard note entering his voice as he essayed tightly, 'A series of thuds like . . . something being hammered into wet wood perhaps?'

Revel's breath caught in her throat. His 'something' was the nails or spikes he had mentioned before, she deduced. Disturbingly, a frowning reconsideration of the sound forced her to grant, 'Well, yes, I guess it could have been.' Then, in extenuation, 'But, as I said, I didn't see anyone, and—and certainly I heard no mention of any such tactic being planned.'

'Yes, well, you may be prepared to give them the benefit of the doubt—as usual,' he bit out derisively, and making her want to cry at the change in his demeanour.

'Unfortunately we can't afford to be so magnanimous. Where we're concerned, it could have far more deadly consequences.'

Revel bit at her lip worriedly. 'So what will you do?' she asked in an anxious voice, easing her feet to the floor. Despondently she surmised that the brief softening in his attitude was well and truly over now.

'Waste a bloody lot of time by having to run a metal-detector over every damned tree in the area that's been marked for cutting!' Tyler snapped furiously as he finally set the ute in motion.

At least that would provide some protection, Revel supposed thankfully, huddling deeper into the rug. A sudden horrifying thought struck her and involuntarily she voiced it aloud.

'Maybe it's just as well I got lost, then, otherwise you might not have known to take precautions.'

'Or, if you'd realised what you'd heard, you wouldn't have mentioned it.'

Revel gasped in a mixture of disbelief, indignation, and sheer mounting anger. 'And if you believe that, then I damn well wish I hadn't mentioned it!' she stormed. 'When have I ever given you reason to think I would be party to something like that?'

'Every time you tacitly give them support by associating with them!' he had no compunction in blazing back. 'By taking part in their efforts this morning to force others to submit to *their* wishes!' His taut features grew mocking. 'It must have been a great disappointment to you when the weather kindly relieved us of the necessity of having to suffer your irresponsible antics.'

Recalling her close shave, Revel was swift to retort with feeling, 'Nearer to grateful would be more like it! And especially since the only reason I was there was so I could talk to Sebastian alone.'

'In order to plan your next strategy?' Tyler gibed, and her hands clenched until her nails dug into her palms as she contemplated physical retaliation.

'I'm beginning to think it would merely serve you right if it had been!'

'Implying it wasn't?'

He made it sound so unbelievable that it was all she could do to answer without losing total control. As it was, her voice rose markedly.

'Not implying, *stating*! As I attempted to tell you before—only you weren't interested in listening—it was solely in order to determine for myself precisely what Sebastian's, and his group's, aims were. Just as *you* suggested I should!' she reminded him on a sniping note.

'And...?' He slanted her an inscrutable look.

Revel sighed and averted her gaze as awareness of her reply seemed to drain her anger, leaving her feeling like an abruptly deflated balloon. 'You were right,' she owned cheerlessly. 'Their objective would appear to be something along the lines of a subsistence culture.'

Tyler nodded, but, somewhat surprisingly, without the least sign of any mockery or gloating that she might have expected. 'So what will you do now? Return to Brisbane with your mother and brother when they leave?' he enquired flatly.

Meaning that was what he wished she would do? Anguish welled up in her chest at the thought. 'I suppose so,' she granted with a sudden uncontrollable huskiness. Then, forcing a concealing half-laugh, 'Although I'll have to pick up my car from the camp first. It appears to have become something of a habit while I've been here, having to collect it from some place or another.'

'Mmm, I guess you have had enough unpleasant experiences to last you for a while. No doubt you'll be pleased to leave them behind when you go.'

In the same way he would be relieved to see the last of her, Revel suspected he meant, and swallowed to try to rid her throat of the aching lump that seemed to have lodged there.

'At least it brought Mum and Hattie in contact with each other again, so it wasn't entirely a waste of time and effort.' Aware that she was coming close to babbling, yet filled with the dismaying premonition that she was going to break into tears if she stopped talking, and praying for the house with its promise of refuge to come into view, she continued quickly, 'And, talking of effort, I haven't yet thanked you for yours in coming to look for me today. One way or the other, I seem to have caused all of you trouble.'

Tyler didn't deny it, she noted, but simply qualified obliquely, 'Well, you certainly brought a new dimension to our lives, I'll give you that.'

Mmm, an unwanted one! Revel bent her head, but thankful beyond belief to have seen them approaching the house as she did so. 'I'm sorry,' she breathed chokingly. 'It wasn't my—I didn't mean ... Oh, we're here!' The exclamation was made in feigned surprise as they drew up close to the door. 'I can't wait to have a shower,' she added excusingly and, hugging the rug to her, she was out of the ute, into the house, and flying up the stairs to her room before Tyler could stay a word.

But, once inside her room, it wasn't for the shower that Revel headed. It was to the bed, where, for the second time in just over a week, she collapsed on to it to give vent to scalding tears. Oh, lord, how had this alienation developed to such an extent? If only she hadn't been so——

'Revel!' Tyler's entry into the room was nothing like Hattie's had been. He burst in like some dark, smouldering force, fragmenting her thoughts and sending her scurrying to her feet. 'What the devil's got into you?' he demanded roughly, his green-flecked eyes surveying her intently as he paced closer. 'Incoherent and subdued just isn't your style.' An inescapable hand abruptly spanned her jaw. 'And why the hell are you crying?'

Revel pulled away from his touch distractedly in a vain attempt to overcome the feeling of helpless vulnerability that was sweeping over her in the face of his flagrant masculinity. He had discarded his hat and oilskin and was dressed in a dark green roll-neck sweater and jeans. By the tousled way his hair curled about his head, it looked as if he had scrubbed a hand through it, and she was assailed by an unnerving urge to run her own fingers through it as well. It lent his face a dangerously boyish quality, when his commanding presence and obvious virility proclaimed that he was every inch a man.

'The—the effects of the day are just catching up with me, I expect,' she stammered defensively at last, clutching the rug in front of her as if for protection rather than covering.

'Bull!' The single word was explicit and unbelieving. 'Don't give me that!'

Revel considered that best ignored. 'Well, anyway, I—I have to shower.' She started to sidle around him, but a hand reaching across in front of her to rest on the wall barred her progress.

'That didn't seem of such concern a moment ago,' Tyler pointed out with a meaningful glance at the bed where she had been lying.

'No, well, my privacy wasn't being invaded then,' she dissembled unsteadily, rubbing at the errant dampness streaking her cheeks. 'And you have no right to be in here. What if Mum or—or Hattie should happen to come past?' An anxious look was cast in the direction of the open doorway.

'I hardly think that's likely since they've all gone visiting old friends . . . remember?'

So they were alone in the house. Revel shifted restively from one foot to the other. 'In which case you have even less right to be in here.'

'No right?' she was startled by Tyler suddenly exclaiming vehemently. 'I've just spent the best part of three hours, in appalling conditions, combing that bloody forest in search of you! I think that at least gives me the right to know why, when we finally arrive home, you take off as if the hounds of hell are at your heels and I find you in tears! Don't you?'

Revel edged the tip of her tongue over her lips. 'B-but you were only looking because of the consequences that might have ensued if——'

'Was I?' he interrupted to counter tautly, capturing her chin with a forceful hand again, and she swallowed convulsively, unsure of just what he was implying.

'You could have felt obliged to, then . . . because of Mum and Quentin being here,' she offered in a tremulous whisper, her eyes wide and shimmering as they gazed uncertainly into his.

Tyler shook his head slowly. 'If you want the truth, I was worried to death about you being out there, particularly after that incident with Jay,' he surprised her by disclosing on a deep note. 'For all I knew, for you to have been close enough for that to happen——' he drew a finger gently down the cut on her cheek in a gesture that made her quiver '—you could also have had concussion, a fracture, anything.' He slid his hands into her hair on either side of her head, his fingers moving caressingly against her scalp, and her quiver became a positive tremble. 'You also asked me once whether I wanted to make love to you, and I said I did.' His head lowered and his mouth brushed one corner of her parted lips. 'I haven't changed my mind.'

Revel moved her head helplessly, feeling herself succumbing—wanting to, so much wanting to—and yet . . . 'But you were so annoyed, and then so distant,' she partly accused, partly puzzled.

That captivating smile of his, which she had missed so much, suddenly caught at his mouth, and had the same effect on her as always. It turned her heart over in her chest and suspended her breathing.

'Well, from my point of view, it *was* beginning to appear as if it wasn't so much the trees you were fighting for, but me you were fighting against,' he murmured, drawing his thumbs along her jawline. His eyes rolled skywards momentarily. 'Unjustified abuse! Sweet heaven, you couldn't have given Renwick's damn group more vindication if you'd tried.'

Revel looked away. 'I know,' she acknowledged miserably. Her eyes lifted to his again. 'But I've already said I was sorry for that.' She hesitated. 'I was just so hurt you wouldn't believe I hadn't told them where you were working. I didn't, you know. I swear I didn't.'

'Then I guess it's my turn to apologise now,' Tyler conceded, touching his lips to the other corner of her mouth. He expelled a sighing breath. 'Maybe if you hadn't been so secretive about your reason for coming here in the first place...'

Revel hunched a deprecating shoulder. 'I don't think I was prepared to take the chance on driving you away,' she confessed throatily. An involuntary shiver shook her. 'Instead I thought I must have alienated you completely and——'

'Uh-uh! My feelings don't change that easily,' Tyler contradicted in thickening tones, covering her face with reassuring kisses. He shook his head. 'Don't you know I've wanted you from the night we first met?' His hands slipped to her shoulders and then to her fingers, which continued clutching the rug between them. 'You also had your arms around my neck when I was carrying you this afternoon. I think I'd like them there again.'

'Oh, Ty...' Revel willingly complied, the rug dropping unheeded to the floor and beneath her feet as he drew her tightly against his hard length. 'I've wanted you, too...so much,' she owned shakily, her breath mixing with his as his lips closed over hers to make her mouth his own.

Within seconds Revel felt her emotions winging out of control as passion, so long restrained, flared between them. Nothing mattered any more except that she was in his arms and he was kissing her as if he never meant to let her go.

His hands traced a tantalising path down to her curving waist and back again, releasing the clasp of her bra, and laying bare her swelling breasts to his caressing fingers. Shivers of pure sensation swept through Revel, and with an aching urgency her own hands slid beneath his sweater to savour the feel of his smoothly muscled flesh.

Swiftly Tyler disposed of the impeding garment altogether, his ensuing sigh of satisfaction mirroring Revel's own as heated skin fused with heated skin. It was a heady feeling to realise his raw need, and she melted against him, weak with longing.

With a groan heavy with desire, Tyler carried her across to the bed, adeptly removing what little was left of her clothing and replacing it with sensuous caresses and inflaming kisses that turned her mindless with wanting. Brief moments later he had removed his own clothes with considerably more haste, and then he was gathering her to him again, his strong, tanned limbs entangling with hers, and his lips possessing hers hungrily before descending leisurely to explore and suckle already hardened nipples.

'Lord, you're irresistible,' he groaned against the sweetly perfumed valley between her throbbing breasts. Lifting his head, he stared down at her with eyes smoky with desire. 'I love you, angel, make no mistake about that.' His breath came raggedly. 'In fact, I love you so damned much, it scares me.'

Languid with passion, Revel's turquoise eyes darkened as she felt her heart expand. 'And I love you with every breath in my body,' she responded adoringly, urging his head up to hers once more, and welcoming the probing, ravishing invasion of his tongue as his mouth reclaimed hers with searing hunger.

Revel moved against him feverishly, and, aware of her peaking desire, Tyler eased her beneath him, pressing into her slowly until he was embedded deep within her and she tightened about him, revelling in the feel of the silken, throbbing warmth that filled her. The strength of him yielding to her was a potent feeling.

Then, soon, Tyler was moving within her, delving deeper with each arousing stroke, and Revel arched to meet him rapturously, eroding his control until he was driving into her without restraint and their bodies surged in unison towards an ecstatic climax that left them shuddering with the force of the unbelievable explosion of feeling that racked them.

For a long time they lay locked together, both of them basking in the afterglow of their union, and both of them a little dazed by its intensity. At last Tyler rolled to his side, propping his head on a supporting hand and looking down at her tenderly. Revel's skin was damp with perspiration, as was his, her eyes drowsy and soft with the wonderment of a love she wouldn't have believed possible, her lips still bearing the signs of their passion as she smiled at him self-consciously.

'You never did tell me why you were crying,' Tyler murmured softly, brushing her hair back from her forehead.

Revel circled her lips with her tongue. 'Because I thought I'd lost you,' she owned simply. 'Because I thought you were looking forward to seeing the last of me.'

Tyler's eyes darkened. 'I never want to see the last of you,' he vowed with all the depth of feeling in his voice that she could have wished, and drawing her back into his arms so that her head was resting on his shoulder. 'In fact, if you're still interested in conservation, I was thinking you might like to stay around—to keep me on the straight and narrow, as it were,' he added idly as he raised her hand to press his lips against her palm.

Revel touched the same hand to his cheek. 'That could be a lifetime's work,' she proposed, adopting the same casual air.

'Mmm, that's rather what I had in mind,' Tyler concurred with another of his heart-stirring smiles, and Revel uttered a sigh of sheer contentment as she gave herself up to the satisfying possession of his shapely mouth once more.

She could recall trying to pass off her attraction to Ty as merely being of a temporary nature, but now she knew beyond doubt that it very definitely had been no passing fancy, after all.

'Well, tonight's the night, hmm?' said Tyler on stepping from the adjoining bathroom into the master bedroom of the house at Mount Winsome with only a towel fastened loosely about his lean hips. 'The moment when all your efforts really come to fruition.'

Deliberating over what jewellery to wear, if any, Revel looked up to smile at him via the dressing-table mirror. 'Oh, I hope so,' she responded expressively.

It was nine months since she had first arrived in Mount Winsome, the last seven of which she and Tyler had been married. Seven of the happiest months of her life, and which had more than made up for any feeling of loss on resigning her position with Ballards. No doubt helped by the fact that those months had probably also been seven of the busiest she had ever experienced, Revel reflected whimsically, as she had set about organising a local conservation group in the town.

Not unexpectedly, at first she had met with a considerable amount of resistance. Although Sebastian's group had eventually departed, when their demonstration had generated no general support, the memories of their protest, and her association with it, had been difficult to overcome.

Nevertheless, with perseverance—and the Corrigan name behind her, she was willing to admit—she had eventually managed to get her message across that it was a balanced approach and improvements through consultation, not confrontation, that she was aiming for, whereupon she had gradually succeeded in gaining the community's interest and trust. So that now, for the first time, their group was to be addressed by a speaker from one of the mainstream organisations, and she was hoping for a big turn-out at the hall in town.

'Although I could never have done it without your help,' Revel added, crossing the room to link her arms lovingly about Tyler's neck and kiss him. 'And not only by teaching me about the forest, so I did know more of what I was talking about, but also by advising me as to who I would need to win over first in order to get the rest to follow.'

Tyler shrugged, but willingly encircled her with his arms. 'I've a suspicion you would have succeeded, anyway,' he claimed lazily. 'I've seen the effect you have on my men alone. You have a way with you of pointing out areas of concern that makes them only too anxious to oblige.' He gave an eloquent laugh. 'Just this afternoon I heard Jay tearing strips off the new dozer-driver for not taking enough care of the surrounding growth as he was putting a new snigging track through.' His hands slid to her shoulders, his fingers caressing the silky skin exposed by her slip as his voice deepened. 'Besides, you should know by now that whatever makes you happy makes me happy.'

Revel pressed closer, her lips trailing a sensuous path across his lightly hair-dusted chest. '*You* make me happy,' she breathed on a deep note. 'I may *like* doing my bit for the environment, but I *adore* you, Tyler Corrigan.'

Anything but immune to the curving form moulded so closely to him, Tyler drew a steadying breath. 'Although you'd better not adore me too much, dressed like that, or we may never make it to your meeting tonight,' he advised drily.

With a shiver of anticipation, Revel eyed him provocatively from beneath her long lashes. 'W-e-ll, it isn't for another hour yet.'

Tyler's mouth tilted. 'Are you flirting with me, Mrs Corrigan?' he enquired in an amused drawl.

Revel dimpled. 'I do my best flirting when I'm scantily clad, Mr Corrigan.' Raising herself on tiptoe, she deposited a lingering kiss against the corner of his mouth. 'Or hadn't you noticed?'

'I notice everything about you, my love,' he groaned resonantly, and capturing her own lips in a kiss that took her breath away before swinging her into his arms and making for the bed. 'You are a delight, and you raise my temperature every time I see you.'

Revel recognised the feeling and her arms tightened about his neck. 'Besides, there's something I've been waiting all day for the right moment to tell you,' she whispered against his ear as he lowered her on to the bed.

'Such as?' he prompted, nuzzling the curve between her throat and shoulder on drawing her back into his arms as he stretched out beside her.

'I went to the doctor this morning and he confirmed what I've suspected for some weeks now,' she relayed with an air of suppressed excitement.

Tyler abruptly pushed himself up on one elbow. 'You're pregnant!' he deduced immediately, and she nodded.

'Are you pleased?' A trace of uncertainty made an appearance in her gaze as her eyes sought his.

'Hell! How could I not be?' As if to prove the point, his ensuing kiss was not only rewarding but extremely thorough. 'Are you?'

'Deliriously!' Revel owned with an ecstatic smile. A sudden and uncontrollable giggle escaped her. 'No doubt Ellis will be, too. He's dying to see this house filled with children.'

Tyler's mouth shaped obliquely. 'Yes, well, I'm afraid he's just going to have to settle for one to start with.'

'Although there will be more?'

'As always, if that's what you want...' he granted huskily, running his hand down her body with a new possessiveness.

Revel sighed blissfully and wound her arms around his neck. 'Right at the moment, all I want is you, my darling husband,' she declared in fervent tones, and Tyler had no hesitation in proving, to their rapturous satisfaction, that their desires were a perfect match.

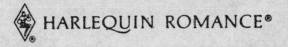

HARLEQUIN ROMANCE®

Norah Bloomfield's father is recovering from his heart attack, and her sisters are getting married. So Norah's feeling a bit unneeded these days, a bit left out....

Orchard Valley

And then a cantankerous "cowboy" called Rowdy Cassidy crashes into her life!

"The Orchard Valley trilogy features three delightful, spirited sisters and a trio of equally fascinating men. The stories are rich with the romance, warmth of heart and humor readers expect, and invariably receive, from Debbie Macomber."

—Linda Lael Miller

Don't miss the Orchard Valley trilogy by Debbie Macomber:

Look for the special cover flash on each book!

Available wherever Harlequin books are sold.   ORC-3

HARLEQUIN®

THE TAGGARTS OF TEXAS!

Harlequin's Ruth Jean Dale brings you
THE TAGGARTS OF TEXAS!

Those Taggart men—strong, sexy and hard to resist...

You've met Jesse James Taggart in FIREWORKS!
Harlequin Romance #3205 (July 1992)

And Trey Smith—he's THE RED-BLOODED YANKEE!
Harlequin Temptation #413 (October 1992)

Now meet Daniel Boone Taggart in SHOWDOWN!
Harlequin Romance #3242 (January 1993)

And finally the Taggarts who started it all—in LEGEND!
Harlequin Historical #168 (April 1993)

Read all the Taggart romances!
Meet all the Taggart men!

Available wherever Harlequin Books are sold.

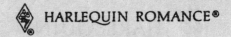

HARLEQUIN ROMANCE®

Some people have the spirit
of Christmas all year round...

People like Blake Connors
and Karin Palmer.

Meet them—and love them!—in
Eva Rutland's
ALWAYS CHRISTMAS.

Harlequin Romance #3240
Available in December wherever
Harlequin books are sold.

HRHX